Praise for *A Double Life*

'Flynn Berry vividly reimagines one of the most notorious crimes of the 20th century. *A Double Life* is a thrilling page-turner, but it is also a compassionate and angry book: with forensic precision, Berry picks apart lives derailed by violence and the ways in which class privilege protect the guilty'

Paula Hawkins, author of *The Girl on the Train*

'What a book! A skilful and compelling exploration of families, crime, and class'

Clare Mackintosh, author of *I Let You Go*

'Beautifully paced and satisfyingly ominous' *Observer*

'Clever, thrilling writing that wound me in and left me heartbroken when I turned the last page and realised it was over'

Fiona Barton, author of *The Widow*

'Confirms the promise of Berry's debut, *Under the Harrow* . . . Mesmerisingly effective' *Sunday Times*

'Flynn Berry writes thrillingly about women raging against a world that protects cruel and careless men. She's less preoccupied by scenes of abuse than the psychological toll of its threat. Her protagonists seethe over their knowledge of violence and are fueled by a howling grief for its victims . . . The ending is as shocking as it is satisfying'

New York Times, Editor's Choice

'[An] interesting . . . reimagining of the Lord Lucan story . . . Berry brings the story to a satisfyingly shocking conclusion'

Guardian

'A compulsive page-turner'   *Daily Mail*

'There are obvious hints of the Lucan case, but Berry makes the story her own, weaving in details that snag at the mind's edge . . . The story dances between rage and compassion. This struggle between opposing values propels the book to its startling conclusion'   *Spectator*

'A damning dissection on class and privilege'
                                        Sarra Manning, *Red*

'Psychological suspense has a new reigning queen'
                               New York Journal of Books

'A detailed and compelling story of a family's fallout from a brutal crime, and the search for truth and retribution'
                               Fanny Blake, *Woman & Home*

'Berry gives the well-worn story of Lord Lucan a fresh twist with this clever tale which tells the story of a woman determined to bring her father's high society friends to justice'
                    i – Independent, Best Beach Reads for Summer

'Thrilling' *Good Housekeeping*, Best New Books for Summer

'Astute . . . With exquisite pacing, Edgar Award-winner Berry guides us to a stunning conclusion'   *Seattle Times*

FLYNN BERRY is a graduate of the Michener Center and has been awarded a Yaddo residency. She graduated from Brown University.

Her first novel, *Under the Harrow*, was awarded the Edgar Award for Best First Novel, and was called 'a triumph' (*Sunday Times*) and 'thrilling' (*New York Times*). *A Double Life* is her second novel. Flynn lives in California.

flynnberry.com

Also by Flynn Berry

Under the Harrow

A DOUBLE
LIFE

FLYNN
BERRY

W&N

WEIDENFELD & NICOLSON

First published in Great Britain in 2018
by Weidenfeld & Nicolson.
This paperback edition first published in 2019
by Weidenfeld & Nicolson
an imprint of The Orion Publishing Group Ltd
Carmelite House, 50 Victoria Embankment
London EC4Y 0DZ

An Hachette UK Company

1 3 5 7 9 10 8 6 4 2

Copyright © Flynn Berry 2018
Published by arrangement with Viking, an imprint of
Penguin Publishing Group, a division of Penguin Random House LLC

A CIP catalogue record for this book is
available from the British Library.

ISBN (Mass Market Paperback) 978 1 4746 0703 2
ISBN (eBook) 978 1 4746 0704 9

Printed in Great Britain by Clays Ltd, Elcograf, S.p.A.
Text designed by Francesca Belanger

MIX
Paper from
responsible sources
FSC® C104740

www.orionbooks.co.uk
www.weidenfeldandnicolson.co.uk

To Robin Dellabough and Jon Berry

After every war
someone has to clean up.

—Wisława Szymborska,
"The End and the Beginning"

CONTENTS

The disappearance of Lord Lucan in 1974 has led to tremendous fascination and speculation.

While the circumstances of the crime in this story were inspired by real life, the characters were not.

They are not based on any of the real people involved, and their personalities, thoughts, and actions are entirely fictional creations.

PART ONE
DOMESTIC

1

A MAN COMES AROUND the bend in the path. I stop short when he appears. The heath has been quiet today, under dark snow clouds, and we're alone on a path where the oak trees form a tunnel.

The man is wearing a hat and a wool overcoat with the collar turned up. When he stops to light a cigarette, I'm close enough to see his knuckles rising under his gloves, but his face is hidden by the brim of his hat.

The dog is somewhere behind me. I don't call for him, I don't want the man to hear. Sparrows fly over our heads to the oaks, drawn into the branches like filings to a magnet. His lighter won't catch, and the metal rasps as he tries again.

Jasper brushes past me, and I reach for his collar but miss, almost losing my balance. The lighter flares and the man tips his head to hold the cigarette in the flame. Then he drops the lighter in his pocket and holds out his fist for the dog to smell. Jasper whines, and for the first time the man looks down the path at me.

It isn't him. I call the dog, I apologize in a strained voice. The path is narrow here, we have to pass within a few inches of each other, and I look at him again, to be sure. Then I clip the dog's lead and hurry towards the houses and people on Well Walk. I wish it had been him, and that instead I was searching the ground for a heavy branch, and following him into the woods.

It's been like this for the past three days, since the detective's visit. I've been seeing him everywhere.

Last Thursday night, I came home from work and ran a bath before taking off my coat. While water filled the tub, I said hello to Jasper, kissing the crown of his head. His fur always smells like clean smoke, like he's recently been near a campfire. I poured a glass of white wine and drank it standing at the counter.

In the bathroom, I filled a small wooden shovel with Epsom salts and tipped them into the water. My friend Nell sent me the salts because they help with aches, she said, and I'm always sore after work. I undressed, listening to the tap dripping in the quiet flat. I left the bathroom door open, since the dog sometimes likes to come and sit next to the tub.

I dropped under the surface, feeling the water slide along the length of my body. I need to suggest massage to Agnes for her arthritis, I thought, then tried to stop thinking about patients. It would help her loneliness, too. Her shoulders relaxed when I checked her heart and she went still, like she was absorbing the touch.

I lay with just enough of my face above the surface to breathe,

the water slipping over my chin. Pasta with pesto for dinner, I decided. A sound came through the liquid, and I raised my head to listen as water spilled from my ears. Someone was ringing the buzzer.

My order, finally, I thought. The book was meant to be delivered two days earlier. I pulled a sweatshirt and tracksuit bottoms on over my wet skin, nudged Jasper back from the door, and ran down the stairs.

There are two doors before the street, and I was in the icy space between them when I saw who it was. Not a courier. The inner door closed behind me. As I opened the next one, the woman lifted her badge. "Do you have a moment to talk, Claire?"

She followed me up the stairs, which seemed to take a long time. My fingers were stiff and I had trouble with the keys. Jasper greeted her, offering her a stick from the towpath. My chest was bare under the sweatshirt, and I left her on the sofa to find a bra.

When I came back, her expression was neutral, but I could tell she'd been studying the room. I wondered what she made of it, and if she'd expected worse, considering my background. It was warm and the lamps were lit. There were books on the shelves, invitations on the fridge, a holly wreath above the mantel. She might have thought I'd made the best of a bad hand.

Or she noticed the open bottle of wine on the counter. The dog, who is half German shepherd, and the number of bolts on the door. It's only at home, I wanted to tell her. I'm not that careful outside. I walk around at night in headphones. I sometimes fall asleep in minicabs, though not often, if I'm honest.

"What's your name?" I asked.

"DI Louisa Tiernan," she said, unwinding her scarf. Her voice was clear and composed, with an Irish accent. The pipes squeaked as the man upstairs turned off a tap. She said, "There's been a sighting."

"Here?"

"In Namibia." DI Tiernan clasped her hands on her knees, but she didn't continue. I didn't understand why she had come. This wasn't news, there have been thousands of sightings.

"Why do you believe this one?"

She handed me an old photograph of my father holding a silver flask engraved with a crest. "Your father bought it at a shop in Mayfair forty years ago. A man has been seen carrying it in Windhoek. He's in his sixties, about six feet tall, and speaks English without an accent."

"Has he been arrested?"

"We're coordinating with Interpol," she said. She looked to be in her forties, which meant she was a teenager when it happened. She must have heard about the case, it was in the news for weeks, and since then has only become more famous. He was the first lord accused of murder since the eighteenth century.

"Why are they waiting?"

"You'll be notified if charges are filed," she said. I wondered if she was surprised to find herself investigating him, after all this time.

"Who told you about the flask?"

"Our source wants to remain anonymous," she said. To avoid the embarrassment, I thought, when he turns out to be wrong. My father has been missing for twenty-six years. People have claimed to see him in almost every part of the world, posting long descriptions of their encounters in the forums about him.

"We hope that you'll be able to help us confirm if it is him," she said. They needed a DNA sample from me. The detective started to explain the process, while my wet hair dripped onto my sweatshirt. I thought of the full bathtub in the other room. I hadn't been out of it for very long, the water would still be warm, the surface perfectly smooth.

The detective put on a pair of surgical gloves. I opened my mouth and she ran the swab against the inside of my cheek, then screwed it into a sterile plastic vial.

"I'm sorry to have to ask," she said, "but has your father ever contacted you?"

"No. Of course not." The curtains were open behind her, and I could see a Christmas tree in the flat across the road. My mouth still tasted like rubber from the glove. I wanted to ask what she would do next, what else she needed to prepare.

After she left, I pulled the plug from the bath, dried my hair, and changed into warm clothes. I boiled water for pasta and opened a jar of good pesto. There was no reason not to eat well, not to watch a show, not to sleep. I didn't need to change my plans, because it wasn't him, it hadn't been any of the other times.

Though the flask is the sort of thing he'd keep, to remind him of the Clermont Club. The click of the lighter, bending his head with a cigarette in his mouth, betting on hands of chemin de fer.

He is a hedonist. That's part of my fury—during all of this, even now, he's somewhere enjoying himself.

———

THE LAST TIME I saw my father was the weekend before the attack. He'd taken me to Luxardo's in Notting Hill. I had a scoop of ice cream covered in coconut, so it looked like a snowball, and my father ordered a peppermint ice cream. It came with a stick of red-and-white peppermint, which he gave to me.

Someone was angry with me that day, a friend of mine from school. I can't remember why now, but I remember how heavily it weighed on me, how bruising it seemed, and I remember how reassuring it was to be with my father.

I've gone over this visit so many times. Him in a dark suit, against the parlour's striped green walls. He had a scratch on the back of his hand; how did that happen? Did he get it during his preparations? I know from one of the forums that the police found a pulped melon at his flat. Since reading that, I've had the idea of him setting a melon on the counter and bringing the pipe down on it again and again, working out how hard he'd need to swing. The idea seems absurd, but no more than the rest of it. Was there a moment—while he was scooping the melon pulp into a bin, maybe, or walking to our house—when he realized what he was doing? Did he almost change his mind?

I've been over all of it, his work and his hobbies and interests, looking for the warnings. He liked bullfights, he took Mum to one in Madrid once. Should that have been a cause for alarm?

He also watched horror films sometimes, but only the ones with good reviews, the ones most people ended up seeing. He didn't seek them out, as far as I know. He said that I didn't need to be afraid of them, he explained the different special effects, he told me it wasn't real blood.

Now everything seems like a warning, but you could do this for anyone. Pick out a few odd interests, a few bad days, and build a theory around it. You could do it for me. You could consider the fact that I haven't moved on as proof of something wrong with me. I'm thirty-four years old and a doctor at a practice in Archway. This shouldn't still consume me, but it never goes away. It's like living in a country where there's been a war. Sometimes you forget; sometimes, on a normal road, in daylight, you're too frightened to breathe; sometimes you're furious that it's fallen to you now to understand what happened, to put it to rights.

But he planned it. He came to our house that night wearing gloves and carrying a length of steel pipe. He'd used a saw to cut the pipe down to the right size, and he'd wrapped gaffer tape around its base so his hand wouldn't slip.

He might have already made the weapon before we sat together in a booth at Luxardo's. It's difficult for me to think about that visit. Not because I could have stopped him, exactly. I was eight years old. But the scene seems grotesque. The little girl, accepting a stick of red-and-white peppermint from him. It's like he made me complicit.

2

M Y PARENTS FIRST MET at the Langham hotel on a Saturday night in 1978. The hotel restaurant had curved banquettes and velvet wall panels, and each table had a small lamp with a pleated red shade. Both of them had arrived with other people. Mum and her fiancé, Henry, were having an argument, and sat with their faces turned down to the large menus.

Her flatmates were going to a party in Covent Garden and then to a nightclub, Annabel's. She'd watched them get ready, sitting on the bed while Christy ironed her hair and Sabrina pulled on a pair of burgundy suede boots that reached to her thighs, leaving an inch of bare leg beneath her skirt.

"Tell me, what do you think," Henry said to the waiter, "between the flank steak and the tournedos?" Faye looked on without smiling. Under the table, she touched her knee, which was covered, disappointingly, in ten-denier tights. After the waiter left, Henry turned to her, expectant, as though he deserved to be congratulated for having been nice to the man.

Right now, her flatmates would be drinking cheap prosecco and laughing, Sabrina pinching the bridge of her nose, like she always did when she laughed. They had put on Lou Reed while they dressed, and now the song was caught in her head. *I said, hey, babe. Take a walk on the wild side.* Faye drummed her fingers on her leg. The restaurant was playing jazz at a low volume. She thought, When was the last time I left somewhere with my ears ringing?

She'd ordered the Dover sole, and when it arrived, she thought, I don't want this, I want chips on the night bus home, I want to be on my own.

Across from her, Henry was twisted in his chair, trying to signal the waiter. Their argument had begun in the cab. Henry had been listing for her, yet again, the reasons for leaving his job and the reasons against. She'd said, "It doesn't really matter, does it? You're not going to retrain as an RAF pilot, you're not going to direct films, what difference does it make which bank you work at?" She hadn't meant to say that. He'd said, "You're an assistant. Not quite setting the world on fire."

Not yet, she'd thought. She worked for a chartered accountant, but wanted a job at a record label. As an education, she went to shows on her own four nights a week, all across London. She checked her watch. Only half past nine. She wondered if she could get into Annabel's dressed like this. Maybe if she kept her coat on. Henry was staring at her. "Another bottle?" he asked. What's the point, she didn't say.

He ordered the Chablis. She'd told him once that it was her favorite. But she'd only said that to be funny, she'd never tasted it before. I'm not like you, she wanted to say, I grew up above a pub, my favourite drink is rum and Coke. Though Henry knew all that. She suspected he was proud of himself for liking her anyway.

"Want to drive down to Arundel tomorrow?" he asked. He never held a grudge. Not fiery enough, not passionate enough, she thought, and sat drinking her wine, answering his questions. She wondered who was chatting up her flatmates right now. She pictured Christy dancing a little as she searched the kitchen for a clean glass, Sabrina leaning out over a windowsill with a man pressed next to her, sharing a cigarette. She folded her hands between her crossed thighs and rocked her foot. Her stomach felt light, her skin flushed. She looked at Henry and said, "I'm going to the toilet." She crossed the floor and turned down a carpeted corridor. She went to the cloakroom and said, "I'm so sorry, I don't have my ticket. It's a tartan coat and a white scarf." The boy handed them to her, without any more convincing.

She wasn't surprised when a man materialized at her elbow, or that he was alone. She'd noticed him earlier, he'd been at the banquette opposite hers. She'd never seen his date's face, only the back of her head, a smooth blond curtain.

He handed over a ticket while she stood to the side, doing up the buttons on her coat. As she climbed the stairs, he fell into step with her.

"I'm Colin," he said.

"Faye."

He took the compartment behind hers in the revolving door. Outside, she was brought up short. Rain drilled the road, and they stood together under the streaming portico. There weren't any cabs in front of the hotel, or down the wet street.

He said, "There's a bar next door."

"Actually," she said, "I'm going to Annabel's."

HAVE I GOT IT RIGHT? I've done so much research, and there's plenty of material. The detective who led the investigation wrote a memoir, my father's friends gave interviews, the police submitted evidence to the coroner. Mum kept diaries, on and off, from when she was a teenager until she died. During their first year together, she wrote in her diary every day, long entries, like she didn't want to miss any of it, even the parts when they weren't together.

The rest of it I've imagined. And with every new piece of information, I adjust my reconstruction. I have to be methodical about this, because somewhere in my research is the explanation.

I've learned a lot about the night my parents met from the people on the forums. They know so much about my family. They know the type of perfume Mum wore, the show we watched the night of the murder, the exact lightbulb in the kitchen that was burned out.

They know that the girl my father was with at the restaurant was named Isabel. He told her he was going to the lavatory and never came back, leaving her with the bill. At the time, she was working for an art dealer for very little money. She gave an interview after the news broke. She must have wanted to talk about it, her close shave.

Mum never saw Isabel's face, only the back of her head. I imagine the girl turning, and Mum seeing from across the room that her face was covered in bruises. But that can't be right. The police interviewed hundreds of people who had known my father. Unless some of them were lying, he didn't have a history of violence.

———

THEY WENT to a Greek taverna on their first date. Mum was still dressed in the clothes she'd worn to the Lanesborough, she hadn't been home yet. They ate stuffed grape leaves and cannelloni and drank carafes of red wine. She added the taverna to his list of enthusiasms, which included cold-water swimming, motorcycles and Belgian Malinois, a breed of very large dog.

They talked about their friends and families. He started to tell a story from when he was a teenager, and she waited for him to annoy her, to sound pleased with himself for having done something that wasn't particularly difficult, like drinking a lot, or being sick in an inconvenient place, or failing an exam.

Instead, as Colin imitated himself as a drunk seventeen-year-old, scooping broken glass from his windscreen off the road, she laughed. He wasn't vain, it seemed, or smug, only warm and straightforward. He finished his story and began shovelling up the last of the cannelloni.

She tried to summon up some sour thoughts about him, the kind that had come so easily with Henry. Your hair needs a cut, she thought, but it didn't work. She couldn't dismantle him, like she had others.

He wasn't perfect, though. Impatient, definitely. And greedy. For food, demonstrably, and other things—drinks, cigarettes, sex. Experience. Not for money, though, if his flat was any indication.

The way Mum described his flat surprised me. My grandparents had a lot of money; I wouldn't have guessed my father ever lived in a place like that. The flat was above a tattoo parlour on Dean Street. With the windows open, they could hear the ink gun. It was small, with uneven floorboards, rusting taps, drawers that neither shut nor opened fully, but had plenty of sunlight, and was right in the centre of things.

She liked a poster he had on his wall of a cyclist on his bike during the Giro d'Italia, eating a bowl of pasta. I think about that poster often. It seems so innocent, like proof that there wasn't always something wrong with him.

3

On Farringdon Road, I reach in my bag for my keys, my wallet, convinced I've forgotten something. I left the gas on, I didn't feed the dog, or lock the door. The bus isn't in sight, I might have time to run back and check.

We're having a meeting, though, about hiring a new practice manager, and I can't be late. I look back across Clerkenwell towards my house, as though I'll be able to tell if something's wrong inside it from here. The bus arrives, and I join the queue to board.

Soon we're crossing the canal. A mile west is Camden Lock, but here the canal is quiet. The narrowboats are moored in ice, and some of them have fir wreaths hanging from their prows.

For the length of the ride, I hold my phone in my hand, to hear if the detective calls. It's Monday now, it's been four days, they must be close to arresting him. I leave the bus at Junction Road in Archway and walk past the newsagent's, the betting shop, the lap-dancing club. In the next window, a man reclines in a chair while a barber brings a straight razor up his neck.

Cold air cuts through the thin fabric of my jumper, and I zip up my coat. I check my phone again. There is a man in Windhoek, the police are going to see him, he might be my father. I don't know how to work out the likelihood. It's supposed to be a beautiful city, which makes the odds stronger. He would have chosen somewhere pleasant.

When I arrive, Laila is outside the practice, pulling a chain through her bike. I wait for her to finish closing the lock. She says, "Pint later?"

"Can't tonight. Wednesday?"

She nods. It will be over by then, another false alarm. The police will have frightened an innocent man, and I'll be in the Old Crown with Laila. She hands me her helmet while she pulls off her yellow cycling smock, then we climb the steps.

Our practice is in an ugly mid-century building with stained carpets and leaking radiators. I'm pleased at how little this bothers me. My father would hate it, I'm nothing like him.

Rahul and Harriet are in the staff kitchen making coffee. None of them know who I really am. We changed our names afterwards, Mum, my brother and I, before moving to Scotland. We chose our surname, Alden, from the roads on an Ordnance Survey map. My brother used to be called Christopher, and I still sometimes call him that by accident, if I'm tired or distracted. He calls me by my old name sometimes too, but not by mistake. He was only a baby when we moved; he grew up with our new names. I think he does it deliberately, since he knows I miss it.

I look around the staff room, at Rahul laughing, Harriet

shaking her head, Laurence coming in the door. Which of you would sell a story about me? If my father is found and stands trial, my name will come out. All of them will be approached. They'll be offered ten thousand, twenty thousand pounds.

A tabloid once offered me a hundred thousand pounds for an interview and promised not to reveal my new identity. I was doing my foundation year at St George's Hospital and barely had enough money for food and rent. I'd give half to charity, and spend the other half on a mint-green Vespa, a winter coat, a year of groceries, the lease on a less grim flat. It was so difficult to turn it down.

Everyone at the practice would be tempted, too. But we've spent so much time together. I've known Rahul's sons since they were born, I was at Harriet's wedding last month. I think they would refuse the press, but they'd talk about it at home and with their friends.

Anton arrives and we follow him into the meeting room. I've thought about telling Laila, but I've waited too long, she'd be hurt that I hadn't before in all these years. The only friend who knows is Nell, though she'll never tell anyone.

After the meeting, I have forty-five minutes for paperwork. I sort through radiology results, blood reports and urine tests from the hospital, marking them as normal or abnormal, noting who needs to be contacted about their results. I read through discharge summaries, call the hospital to set up more tests for three of my patients, and send another's medical history to an allergist. I sort through the messages from pharmacists, social workers and district nurses, working out which need responses now and which can wait for a few hours, and then it's eight thirty and I'm opening the door to my consulting room.

My first patient has bronchitis. Then I see a boy with an ear infection, and a new mother who's been having pain while breastfeeding. The next patient is my first new one this morning, a forty-eight-year-old man who says he's been feeling tired. We talk about the fatigue, and I take down his history. I start to ask about his family's history, which is when he says his sister died three months ago. "Oh," I say. "Oh, I'm so sorry." His face slackens, and we sit together until he's able to talk again. I'm late from then on, though everyone seems remarkably tolerant this morning.

None of my patients can learn about my family. I know what it's like. I remember the school playground, after the other girls found out. We're adults now, but the basic responses would be the same. Some of them might not want me as their doctor anymore.

I've only told one boyfriend, when I was at university. We were at a café in Edinburgh, at a table outside in the sunshine. I don't know why I started on it. We'd spent every night of the last week together, my defences were down.

He laughed at first, and then, as I went on, he stiffened. The waiter arrived with our breakfast. Two lattes and a plate of cornettos filled with apricot marmalade. I started to eat, he didn't. The pastry broke apart, the marmalade pooling on my plate. I continued to talk between mouthfuls. At one point, marmalade dripped down my thumb, and I licked it off. He looked at me with distaste, as though I wasn't allowed that gesture anymore.

After work, I walk to get the Northern line instead of the bus home. On the platform, I search for my father on the Interpol site. His name appears on their fugitive list, along with old pictures of him and a police sketch of how he may have aged. I study it, even though I've had the profile memorized for years.

I haven't told my brother about the sighting. Robbie doesn't need to know unless it turns out to be true; he wouldn't cope well with the disappointment.

The train still isn't in sight, but I can hear it in the tunnel, and I step to the platform edge. The rails start to shiver, like hundreds of needles are falling on them.

I change at Euston, and stay on the tube until Victoria. As the train glides into the station, I stand at the doors, facing my reflection—tired face, fringe, the rest of my dark hair up in a knot.

I haven't been back to our old house often. It's not hard to avoid, on a quiet street in Belgravia. I stop at the top of the road and look down the row of terraced houses. Nothing about it seems to have changed. Hooked streetlamps, tall white homes, each with a black number painted by the door. I walk past ours. Someone else lives there now. The property always sells quickly, despite its history.

The entrance is raised from the street by a few steps, and below the steps is a window into the basement. The kitchen is at the back, with doors opening onto the rear garden.

I walk to the pub on the corner, the Blacksmith's Arms. It has the same row of copper lamps above its window, the same hanging sign.

That night, twenty-six years ago, the door opened and a woman ran into the pub. The room fell silent as she stood panting on the threshold. The woman was wearing a dress and stockings, and she was covered in blood.

Her throat and chest were glazed red. She was wearing a headband, and it and her pale hair were stained. Wet handprints tracked over her dress, and parts of the fabric were soaked through, plastered to her stomach tight enough to show her gasping. When she opened her mouth, her teeth were stained black, and blood rolled down her chin.

No one in the pub moved. She tried to speak but couldn't. She started again.

During the attack, my father reached his hand into Mum's throat. At the time, it hurt so much that she thought he'd punctured it, she was feeling for the wound on her neck in the ambulance.

She fought him. He almost killed her, but she got away, and ran to the pub on our corner. She didn't know then what my father had already done.

Emma had been living with us for nine months. After our father left, Mum hired her to help look after us. They looked similar. They were both slim, with fair hair, though Emma's was light brown and Mum's was ash blond.

One of the lights in the kitchen was out. My father wouldn't have been able to see the woman clearly before he started to beat her.

I want to know when he realized he'd made a mistake. And why he didn't stop.

He must have some guilt over Emma. He'd planned to kill Mum, not her. I wonder what he has done to atone. If he has confessed to a priest, wherever he is. I think he would enjoy the process of expiation. I expect he would think that he could be forgiven, that really he already has been.

*

My father's friends said that Mum was wrong. The hallway had been dark, she'd received blows to her head, she was in shock. She couldn't have seen the man's face. My father was innocent, they said, and a burglar, maybe, or one of Emma's former boyfriends had broken into the house.

Or, they said, Mum wasn't confused, she was lying, and had staged the attack to frame my father. They were about to begin divorce proceedings, she might have lost the house, custody, access to his money. "She wasn't stable," said James, in an interview with the *Telegraph*. "You have to understand that. None of us ever knew why he was with her."

4

A FEW WEEKS after they started dating, my father invited Mum away for the weekend to meet his friends. James was waiting to collect them at the village train station in Sussex, leaning against a battered Land Rover, polishing his glasses on his shirt. "Hello," he said. "You must be Faye."

She laughed. She thought he was putting on a cut-glass accent to be funny. He frowned, and she said, "Yes, yes, nice to meet you."

They drove through the village, past a church, a few houses, and onto a narrow lane between hedgerows. The lane wasn't wide enough for two cars to pass, but James didn't brake at the bends. They drove past a herd of sheep, their coats marked with red paint. The paint was meant to show ownership, but made the sheep look like they'd been shot.

Colin said, "How has it been so far?"

"Sam's already made someone leave." He's still doing the accent, thought Faye. That might in fact be his voice.

"Who?"

"Michael. Sam made a joke about his girlfriend. She stayed."

Branches scraped her door. A passing car had to veer into the hedge to avoid them, and the driver sounded his horn. It began to rain. They drove through woodland until James stopped at a gate mounted with two stone lions. Once they were through the gate, Faye looked back to watch it close. They started down a long drive with acres of land on either side. Ahead of them, a house appeared and disappeared as the wipers crossed the windscreen.

She'd never seen a house like this. Or, actually, she had. Her class had been on a school visit to Chatsworth once. This was nearly as large, and made of the same yellow stone. My friend's house in Sussex, he'd said, and she'd pictured something suburban and small. Faye hoisted her bag onto her shoulder and followed Colin to the door. Wet gravel rolled under her feet, and the trees on the lawn thrashed in the wind. High above them, water streamed from the flat roof and fell for a long time, past carved windows and pillars, before reaching the ground.

Faye stood dripping in the front hall. There was a pile of luggage against the wall, and cases of wine. She'd brought a bottle of wine too, though from a petrol station.

The front door opened behind them, and Faye turned to see a woman in a pale trench coat. "Where did you go?" asked James.

"We ran out of tonic," she said. "Hi, Colin." They kissed on the cheek. She had glossy, clean blond hair and a neat, delicate face. Faye stepped forward and the woman said, "Hello, I'm Rose."

"Thank you for inviting me."

Rose turned to the men and said, "Can you get the cases from my car?" To Faye, she said, "We're eating in an hour. Want to drop your bags upstairs?" Faye followed her up a wide staircase and into a large guest room. She couldn't think of anything to say, though she wanted to make a good impression. Colin had told her that Rose was like his sister, and had been with James since they were all fourteen.

After Rose left the room, Faye turned out the lights so she could see through the window. Acres of dark lawn, then woods, and a hill in the distance. No other houses. She could make out the shape of a barn, and a swimming pool. The pool had its underwater lights on, and they dimmed and brightened as the water slid back and forth in the rain.

She studied the small woodcut of the house above the dresser. Ashdown, said the frame. She tested the duvet. She opened the bottle of neroli oil next to the bed—never heard of it, she thought—and sniffed. Then she went into the bathroom, which had a Victorian slipper tub in front of a window, took off her wet coat and socks, and turned on the taps.

From the hot bath, she could hear the cold rain falling on the property. She was still in the bath when Colin came in. He kissed her, then went into the bedroom to rummage through his bag. From the bath, she said, "Colin. Did you grow up in a house like this?"

"Yes."

"You don't have their accent."

"I used to."

He'd told her he went to boarding school, but she'd assumed on a scholarship. She couldn't remember what had made her think so. His flat, maybe. He'd told her a bit about his parents, too, and now she had to revise her image of them. It was an effort, changing out the backdrop of all the stories he'd told her about his childhood, and it didn't really work. She couldn't picture him at four or eleven or fifteen, in a house like this. That would be a completely different person.

She used her foot to add more hot water to the bath. He probably went to one of those schools. Harrow, or Rugby, or Westminster. "Colin. Where did you go to school?"

"Eton."

Her eyebrows lifted. "Did you like it?"

"Yes. Very much." He came to stand in the doorway.

"What was it like?"

"It was fun. Did you like your school?"

"No," she said.

He started to tell her about Eton, but part of her still expected him to say he was joking. "I'm surprised we weren't expelled," he said. "We once took all the furniture from the headmaster's room and assembled it on the lawn."

"Did you?" she said. Two boys had been expelled from her school. They'd torched the science block.

In the other room, Colin's belt clattered to the floor as he stepped out of his trousers. He'd told her his father taught history. Which he did, but as a sort of hobby, apparently, not for the salary. She'd thought Colin was confident because he'd been thrown into a different world at boarding school. Not a different world at all, as it turned out. His.

They ate dinner in a formal dining room. Nine of them at a long table, with candelabras and full place settings, most of which they didn't use. Rose set pans of lasagne down the centre of the table. The room was noisy with conversation, and Faye talked mostly to Rose, who was not at an auction house, as she'd guessed, but a barrister. And funnier than she'd expected, more acerbic.

After dinner, they left their dirty plates on the table. Faye had noticed women around the house, in blue linen shirts. She lifted her plate to carry into the kitchen, and Colin said, "Leave it, it's fine."

In the morning, Faye turned over in bed and looked out the window. It was still early. Mist rose from the lawn and the swimming pool and the woods, but the sky was clear, and the day would be warm. The property was even larger than she'd thought last night, in the dark. Like a feudal estate. White sheep were scattered across the vast green lawn.

Each part of the landscape seemed to be in the exact right place, like in a frontispiece map in a book. There was even a Neolithic dolmen on the hill in the distance. The view made her nervous, like she'd done something she shouldn't have and was about to be caught.

In front of the flint-and-stone stables below, Shetland ponies were grazing in a paddock. Of course they had horses. Did Colin know how to ride? Had he ever been hunting? It didn't seem like the man she knew, who had been with her two nights ago drinking snakebites in a pub in Camden. She turned around to ask, but he was still asleep.

The mist was starting to thin, and sunlight sparked off a wine glass left by the pool. Now she noticed other glasses, and bottles, and sodden towels. They must have gone swimming in the rain last night after she went to bed.

After breakfast, Faye walked with Colin and James down the lawn. They passed through a gap in the hedge wall and onto the tennis court hidden inside. James took racquets from a small blue-and-white-striped spectator's hut.

Faye watched them play for a while, until they both had a skeleton of sweat on their shirts, then wandered outside the hedges. A few of the others were by the pool, asleep on sun loungers or reading. Behind her, she could hear the tennis ball being hit back and forth.

It wasn't so bad, she thought. You couldn't tell, most of the time. Though she had noticed that when they talked about travel, they didn't talk about countries, or towns, or even restaurants, but about specific drinks and dishes, since they'd all been to the same places so many times. The bellini at a certain restaurant in Positano, for example. Apparently it was made with a cold peach slurry.

They'd also all had altitude sickness, which Faye found odd. They talked about it at dinner, how the sickness gave them strange dreams. She wouldn't have thought so many of them would be interested in mountain climbing. "Where do you hike?" she asked. "Not hiking," said James, after a pause. "Skiing."

No one seemed to mind, though. All of them were friendly towards her. Because of Colin, she thought. She noticed that when his friends spoke to the group, they looked at Colin. And he was never interrupted, unlike Sam, who could rarely finish a sentence. Before dinner, they had all hesitated for a moment, just

long enough to let Colin choose his seat first. He'd told her before
that he liked to sit facing the restaurant, and she'd said, "Everyone
does."

At first she'd thought they deferred to him because he was
clever, funny and magnetic, but maybe it was because he out-
ranked them. He would be an earl, he'd told her this morning,
when his uncle died. James would be a viscount, which wasn't
quite as good, and the others wouldn't inherit titles. When she'd
asked, "Will you use the title? Will you make everyone call you
Lord Spenser?" he'd laughed. "Do you really think I'd do that?"

She leaned against the paddock fence and looked at the ponies. Earlier, Rose had said she learned how to ride when she was
three, with her mum walking beside her. She'd had a miniature
Clydesdale pony. Faye had looked around the breakfast table and
wondered what it did to you, to grow up with everything you want.
Colin never had a miniature Clydesdale, as far as she knew, but he
did have a tree house, he'd told her after breakfast, on a corner of
his family's estate. It had windows, a roof, and two levels inside.
So an actual house, then.

She turned away from the paddock and headed towards the
pool. He'd grown up with servants. Staff, he called them. Someone
else had made his bed. Colin had been such a relief after Henry,
she'd thought he was like her.

Rose's friend Orla sat on the edge of the diving board in an
orange bathing suit, talking with Sam. Faye was wary of Sam.
He was friendly, but often said cruel, belittling things, especially
when drinking. She walked past the hedge wall. On the other side,
Colin was arguing with James about a serve. She was near enough
to hear his ragged breathing. I can make a decision, she thought. I

don't have to picture him with servants, or in the first-class cabin of an aeroplane. I can think of him growing up in a small house in Norfolk, bicycling around, doing chores, growing bored, asking to go out for lo mein on his birthday, studying for a scholarship, being nervous in the interview. No one will know if I keep that version, she thought. It fits with who he is now, anyway. He's not spoiled, it may as well be true.

5

I REMEMBER MUM SWIMMING in the pool at Ashdown, and helping to carry bottles of wine out to the long table set on the
terrace. She never showed any signs of unease. She always seemed
to belong in the group of adults, though her accent was different
from theirs.

We visited Ashdown often. There were twenty bedrooms upstairs, and I remember standing at the end of the corridor, certain
that one of the doors was about to creak open. So many people
had lived there, might still be there as ghosts.

The land around the house was also bewitching. The stables,
the woods, the walled garden with its peach, quince and plum
trees. Hundreds of years before, they'd lit fires inside the wall to
keep the fruit trees warm in the winter. I sat inside the disused
fireplaces and read or played imaginary games, always set in a
medieval autumn, with Rose and James's daughter Alice, who was
nearly my age.

I wish now that I hadn't spent so much time there on my own, in the garden or the woods. I wish I'd been in the house, with the adults, listening. Then I might have understood why they hated my mother. They must have, Rose, James and Sam, or they wouldn't have helped my father escape.

I saw Rose on the street once, on a warm evening in June, three weeks after I finished medical school. She was wearing pumps and a shift dress and carrying a jacket over her arm, and she looked like any of the other hundreds of women on their way home from work.

I followed her. I'd spent so much time thinking about her, and then there she was, holding a bottle of mineral water, waiting to cross the road. She turned, her face in profile, to check the oncoming traffic. I was just behind her, close enough to see the redness rubbed into her shoulder by the strap of her bag.

I followed her down Cadogan Street, wondering if she had been in court that day. I looked at the back of her head and the posts of her earrings. The streetlamps hadn't come on yet, but the evening sunlight filled their dusty glass domes so they glowed. Rose lifted her head, like she'd noticed it too.

As we crossed Sloane Square, her phone rang. "Oh, hi, darling. How did the exams turn out? . . . Did he? . . . Right . . . *Right* . . . Are you still coming at seven? . . . Thai, your father's picking it up . . . No, the new place. Call and tell him what you'd like." I knew Alice was in a master's program in California, she must have been back for a visit. Rose laughed. "Don't say that. See you soon."

She turned onto St Leonard's Terrace. The road was quiet, and I stopped on the corner while she took out a key and opened a gate. I waited until she'd gone inside, then stood for a while looking at the house. It was a large townhouse covered in ivy with a fanlight over the door. I've thought about it a lot since then, about the three of them having dinner at home, and the other things they might do as a family.

For a long time afterwards, I fantasized about joining their staff. There was the townhouse in London and the mansion in Sussex. Both residences were large, they would need a lot of help. I would be allowed into all of their rooms as a cleaner. I could eavesdrop, I could find out where my father had gone. But there weren't any open positions in the city or the countryside. The Frasers had a permanent staff, all of whom had worked for them for years.

I decided to focus on James instead. After my father's disappearance, when his friends were often in the press, there were rumours that James visited prostitutes. During the investigation, a woman who worked out of a flat behind King's Cross said he was a former client, and in his diary the police found the address of a condemned building in King's Cross.

James said a friend of his who developed property was considering buying it. No, he didn't use the building to meet a prostitute, he said. He'd never paid for sex in his life.

I've spent so many hours trying to find this woman. Only her first name was ever published, and it might not have been real. She said he'd been a regular client, until he started to make her nervous. He knew she didn't live in the King's Cross flat and wanted to know her address. She thought he'd followed her home once. He started bringing her gifts, things that he wanted her to wear or things to eat, including an expensive set of jams.

I don't know how to find her. If I ever do, though, if I ever find proof, James might agree to tell me where my father went. He's constructed the sort of public life that wouldn't withstand that exposure. He's a major donor to the Conservative party, which would distance itself from him, the private causes he supports would remove him from their boards, his firm would fire him.

For three months that summer after medical school, I followed James to his members' club in Mayfair, and to Waterloo station, where he caught the train down to Sussex. I watched him buy clothes, read newspapers, have his hair cut. He often went for massages, but always at the same expensive day spa.

I followed him to his office at an insurance firm near the Royal Exchange. He took at least a full hour for lunch, often at Sweetings. The restaurant was always full of men in suits. Cracked paint on the walls, wood trim, cartoons of politicians. It seemed grotesque, the still life of pheasants strung up by their necks, the smell of fish, the bright lights on all those men eating sandwiches filled with glistening white crabmeat. He usually went with the same colleague. They ordered crab sandwiches and a bottle of Meursault. When I could sit within earshot, their conversations were mostly about work, or politics, or travel, nothing useful. The problem was that James travelled so often for work, and I couldn't follow him on his business trips. I had no way of knowing what he did when he was out of town.

Early one morning, I watched him get out of a black cab and wheel a suitcase to the door. He'd been to Hong Kong for work,

I'd overheard him telling his colleague about the trip. The suitcase still had a yellow airline tag attached. He had trouble finding his key, and I heard him sigh. He must have been jet-lagged. I was so tired of waiting. I wanted to walk up to him and say, Was it a good trip? What did you do to relax?

I stopped watching him soon after that, out of frustration, and because my schedule changed so drastically. Once my foundation year began, I was always at the hospital, or collapsing into bed after a night shift.

Sam and Orla separated six years ago. I hoped then that she would decide to tell the truth; I'd read an interview with a Met detective who said that half of his cold cases were solved after a divorce. But Orla didn't go to the police, as far as I know. She did convert to Catholicism, though.

Sam has dated a lot of women since then. I'm not his type, but could probably approximate it with enough effort. Something in my mind closes down, though, when I even consider it.

I haven't followed any of my father's friends in years, but I'm still watching them. I clip the pictures of them that sometimes appear in the paper after parties or charity dinners or gallery openings. I recently watched a short, blurry video of Sam at a wedding, using a sabre to cut open a bottle of champagne.

I know the names and addresses of their members' clubs. I know the names of their children and their godchildren, of which they each have about ten, some of whom have public profiles online. I know from *The Times* that Sam's neighbours in Chelsea were annoyed by the constant building work while he combined two adjacent houses. The house number in the picture was blurred, but I circled through Chelsea until I found his street. Watching them has become more a habit than anything else. I don't know what might change and finally tear an opening for me to come inside.

6

ON SUNDAY, I need to leave my flat. The detective still hasn't called, and the waiting is making me skittish. I've been thinking so much about how they'll arrest him, this man who might be my father, how they'll break into his house, find the room he's in, force him to the floor. I didn't ask DI Tiernan if the man lives alone. My father might have a wife now, or other children; they might be about to learn who he is.

I can't hold my hands steady. I was too frightened to close my eyes in the shower this morning, which hasn't happened in years. I have to remember to swallow, and when I do the sound startles me. I don't know why this is happening. I'm not in any danger. But I've already dropped and broken two cups, and while I was on my knees, gathering the shards and mopping the liquid, I had to check that there wasn't a man behind me, ready to shove me back down if I tried to stand up.

I keep thinking that he's going to shoot himself. He'll lock the door, go into another room, and lift a gun before they can arrest him. It's part of why I can't stay still now. The blast might happen at any moment. It might have already happened. The thought makes me furious, with the thwarted, heaving rage of a tantrum.

I call Laila. "Are you free today?" I ask, my voice desperate. "Do you want to get together?"

"Sure," she says, yawning, and my shoulders lower from around my ears. We plan to meet at the Holly Bush in Hampstead. I've just left the house, I'm still on Sekforde Street, when my phone rings. I can't find it and crouch down on the pavement, using both hands to dig through my bag. It's Rahul, asking if I can cover his on-call shift this week. I agree, and then stay in a crouch, my face in my hands.

On the tube I sit with my eyes closed, the train rattling beneath me, thinking, It's not him, it hasn't been any of the other times.

When I come up from the station in Hampstead, the high street is crowded with people looking in the shop windows, carrying suits out of the dry cleaner's, waiting in a long queue to buy crepes from the stand across the road. The sight leaves me dazed, after the quiet of my flat. More people come and wait near me at the crossing. I step back from the buses as they pass, like someone might shoulder me under them.

The Holly Bush is tucked away in a bend in the road on the hill above the high street. Laila is at a table near the fireplace. She kisses me hello, and as I sit, she says, "What's wrong?"

"Nothing, why?"

"You look—" she says, and stops, her eyes on my face.

"Tired? I didn't sleep well last night."

"Is it Robbie?"

"No," I say, which isn't entirely true. I'm always worried about my brother. And I feel uneasy for not telling him about the detective's visit, he'll be furious with me if he finds out I kept it from him. "I just couldn't fall asleep. Are you hungry?"

She orders the roast chicken, and I order a vegetable Wellington. I ask Laila about her weekend, and we talk about work. She's thinking of opening her own practice somewhere rural, or becoming a locum. When she goes outside to answer a call from a district nurse, I look around the pub at the wooden beams on the ceiling, the fire, the other people in the room, the white mistletoe berries, like thin-skinned pearls.

We order plum pudding, which comes with a ramekin of brandy butter to pour on top. I'm absorbed in this task, but the thoughts—do they have him, have they arrested him—are just as insistent as when I was alone in my flat. This always surprises me, how it's possible to be entirely occupied by two things at once, and how little they can have in common.

We say goodbye outside the tube station. Instead of going straight home, I decide to cross the heath and get the bus from Highgate. Bare black trees arch over the path, and the ground is rutted and frozen. I can feel the warm tip of my nose in the cold air.

Past the edge of the field, Highgate rises on a hill. A church spire, some roofs and chimneys between the trees, like a country village. I continue towards its spire, the frozen ground creaking under my boots. My phone will ring while I'm here, I think.

It starts to snow. Only lightly, but enough to begin to turn the fields and paths white. I keep walking as snow drifts over the trees, and my face feels tight and clean in the cold. I start to think about what I will say to him.

7

"Y OU CAN STILL change your mind," my grandfather said to Mum over the birdsong and crickets. A tractor engine stopped and started somewhere in the distance.

She yawned. "Do you think we have time?"

An usher would open the door soon. There were already two hundred guests inside, the families were being seated. When Colin had said there was a chapel on his family's estate, she'd pictured something the size of a shepherd's hat, but this was as large as the church in her town. Its door was studded with nails, which Faye tested for sharpness with her finger. Gene pulled at his tie. He'd worn his own suit instead of renting a tailcoat. "Oh dear," Deborah, Colin's mother, had said when she saw him.

Faye beat her bouquet against her leg. The sun was warm on her back and shoulders, and butterflies twitched above the meadow. A saddle hung over a fence. "Do they hunt?" asked Gene.

"What do you think?"

Colin's family was "horse-mad", especially Deborah. On her first visit, Faye had lifted a polished object from a side table. "What is this?"

"My grandfather made it," said Deborah. "When his favourite horse died, he turned her hooves into inkwells." Faye tried not to think about the mechanics involved in the process.

The usher opened the door and nodded at them. Faye pulled the veil over her head so it hung before her face. Its hem reached to her chest, weighted by a line of broderie anglaise. She hadn't wanted to wear it, but every bride in the Spenser family had for the past two hundred years. Her father took her arm and they climbed the stone steps. Faye felt the sun on her back, and the cold air of the church on her front. The veil fell against her face as she walked, and she imagined that she looked like she was emerging from under water.

When she arrived at the altar, Colin was smiling at her, and she knew he was thinking the same thing, that no one had found them out. They'd already been married for a year. They'd married at a registry office in Chelsea, two months after meeting at the Lanesborough. Faye had worn a suede miniskirt and high boots. She'd carried a bunch of lilies of the valley, their bells tolling as she walked.

After the second ceremony, Colin said, "Am I technically a bigamist now?" The wedding party crossed the wide lawn to the marquee. The tent was white, with three pennants. Faye took a flute of champagne. With its pennants, the tent looked like the camp of an invading army. Which would be her, she supposed.

Rose kissed her. "Well done," she whispered, and the two of them huddled amidst the circling waiters, who were passing glasses of chilled prawns and king crab legs. She drank more champagne, enjoying the party as though she were a guest. At one point, she went into the house with Sabrina and Christy, and they lay side by side in a canopy bed drinking brandy alexanders.

"The first year of marriage," said James in his toast, "is the most difficult. But I think there's a good chance that at the end of it, you'll be just as happy as you are today." He knew, of course. He'd been one of their witnesses at the registry office in Chelsea.

The waiters served chicken poached in milk, then a cake with thick fondant etched to resemble lace. At her real wedding, they'd had a croquembouche, a tower of profiteroles in a sticky caramel glaze.

During the dinner, Faye felt private and removed. She noticed a wooden gate someone had left unlatched at the end of the property, and watched it blow back and forth in the wind.

"Did you go to Bedales?" asked one of the guests.

"No," said Faye. "I went to a comprehensive school in Stafford."

"Oh, well done, you," said the woman. "Did you also attend university in the Midlands?"

"I didn't go to university. I wanted to start working."

"And where do you work?"

Faye looked at her and thought, She wants to know if we signed a prenup. She considered just telling her. Colin's family had insisted, and Colin refused, which was good, because they'd already been married for a year without one.

A group of guests surrounded her and asked for the story of how they met. They expected more, thought Faye. They expected a great beauty.

"He picked me up at a restaurant," she said.

After a pause, one of them said, "And you've been together ever since," in a tone of wonder.

Tomorrow night they'd be back at the flat on Dean Street. They would have sex, and have a shower. He would put on a record, and she would wear one of his jumpers and the pair of soft knee-high socks he'd bought for her to wear at home. They would cook pasta with tomato sauce and drink a bottle of wine. They would read or talk or project a film on the wall, and she'd sit against him, cradling the glass on her stomach, her socked legs folded.

Faye left the guests to find her father, and they sat alone in a corner talking about his pub. "I've made some improvements," said Gene.

"Oh Christ, no," said Faye. For a while he'd had Free Tuesdays. It had not been a good idea.

Colin was across the tent, talking with James, his hands in his pockets. James shook his head, ran a hand through his hair. Faye wanted to hear what they were saying. Across the room, Colin closed his eyes, like he was wincing. She wasn't the only person watching them. She'd noticed that before with Colin. At large dinners, people a few seats down would stop eating and lean over to listen to him.

Colin left James, and a moment later he appeared beside her with a bottle of wine and glasses for her and her father. He kissed Faye, checked his watch, and said, "When can we ask them all to leave?"

"Well," said Deborah, once the guests were gone. "That was a success." She had arranged for them to borrow her friend's house in Provence for their honeymoon.

"Actually," Faye had said, "we're going to India."

And on their honeymoon a week later, in a coracle spinning on a river in Hampi, Faye gripped the straw edges of the boat and she laughed and laughed and laughed.

———————

AFTER THEY WERE MARRIED, my parents often went on trips abroad with his friends, to rented villas in France, Sardinia, Mallorca. I visited the one in Mallorca when I was twenty-two, after saving for months to buy the ticket.

I went in September, when the villa where they'd stayed was empty. A sign for a security system was posted on a fence in front, but I opened the gate and walked around the house to the pool. Cicadas rasped in the tall weeds. Lemons had fallen from the trees and lay scattered in the grass.

I was sick from the bus ride across the island, and picked a lemon from a tree next to the pool. Mum was pregnant with me when they came here, and had terrible morning sickness. She wrote in her diary that she tore lemons open with her hands and sucked on the juice. Apparently it helped with the nausea. My incisors dug into the rind, and the juice ran down my hands, burning on the raw skin around my nails. I pulled my teeth from the peel, feeling like a vampire. She was right, it did help.

The villa was on a cliff above the water. I walked down its steep stairs and out onto a rickety wooden jetty. When I finished drinking its juice, I threw the lemon in the water, where it floated on the surface, caught in the foam beating against the rocks.

Mum didn't have an easy pregnancy, between her morning

sickness, which was bad enough that she had to be hospitalized a few times for fluids, and her fear at how much would change. She'd become pregnant by accident, after the antibiotic she was prescribed for strep throat interacted with her birth control. My father was excited. During their trip, he went to the market in Deià and bought a wooden rattle painted with horses for me.

I was so tired. I'd booked the cheapest flight, which meant being at the airport at four in the morning. Before coming to the villa, I'd stopped at the hostel to shower and change into a navy dress with short sleeves. I'd chosen the dress carefully, because a part of me had expected to see Mum again here, like that would be my reward for having come this far. I'd pictured her looking up when she heard me and smiling, saying my name, my real name. Standing from the jetty and holding out her arms to me.

The empty jetty creaked as waves passed beneath it. I was crying now, though part of me still hoped that if I couldn't see her, maybe I could at least feel something, a presence, that she might still comfort me somehow. After a long time, I wiped my wet face and leaned forward to dip my arms in the cool water. It was no use, she was gone.

From the jetty, the water was so clear it looked gelatinous. Two boats anchored in the cove seemed suspended in air, above their shadows on the seabed. I could see the green and white barnacles on the rocks under the surface.

Mum went snorkelling here. She told me once that she'd loved swimming when she was pregnant, with her stomach below her in the water, like a submarine.

If I had been on this jetty twenty-three years before, I would have seen her. The snorkel rising from the water as she swam farther out into the cove, the black flippers, the length of her body, her shadow following her, slipping over the rocks.

That night I went to the bar attached to my hostel. A table of backpackers invited me to join them, then we went to another bar. I walked next to Nick, who was from Australia, who was wearing a faded yellow shirt, who was teasing me the right way, affectionately, like we'd known each other for longer. I pretended that I hadn't noticed his group before, that I hadn't gone down to the common area hoping they would be there.

At the second bar, we drank beers and shots of tequila. Nick put his hand on my leg while making a point, then left it there when he looked across the table to answer one of his friends. When we went to the bar to order more drinks, he held me around the waist, and I took him into the washroom.

On the bus to the airport, I thought about the sex over and over, like it had been the real purpose of the trip.

8

M Y PHONE DIDN'T RING on the heath. When I get home, I'm
chilled and shivering. Jasper starts to whine when he hears
my keys. I drop to the floor and he bows the top of his head against
my chest while I scratch the soft fur behind his ears. The radiators
hiss steam. Outside, the snow has stopped, and low bruised clouds
are suspended over the city. I run a hot shower, and I'm still under
the water when my phone starts to ring.

"Claire," says DI Tiernan, in a careful, measured voice, as I
stand dripping in the living room. My hand is over my mouth,
and I'm almost smiling. A lightness is already swelling up from my
legs, and I'm about to bow my head, press my hand to my chest,
say, Thank you, say, What will happen now?

She says, "I'm so sorry."

After the call ends, I set the phone down and stare across my
flat. "He looked so much like your father," she said. "We didn't
know until the DNA results arrived."

Jasper's lead is curled on the table. I have to remember to pay the dog walker tomorrow. This is the worst part, always. How difficult it is to return to my daily life, how impossible to fit back inside it, after a false alarm. I know, from the past, that for the next few weeks everything will be an effort. I'll have to write lists to remember to do even the most obvious things. And this time will be worse, I think. It's been longer since I've gone onto the forums or searched for his friends' names. I thought I'd made progress.

I go back into the bathroom and take the can of pepper spray from its hiding place behind a row of shampoos and soaps. It's illegal here. I order the cans online once a year and they arrive in an unmarked box. I've often wondered if I would be able to reach it in time. If, after hearing someone open the bathroom door, I'd be able to aim it before my head was cracked against the wall. I pick up the canister and thrash it against the side of the tub until the metal dents and crumples.

WORK HAS BEEN difficult today. My first patient of the morning had appendicitis, and I had to wait with her for the ambulance, and talk to a doctor at the hospital, and send on her history, which put me twenty minutes behind for the rest of the morning. Our practice manager told me a patient had filed a complaint about me for always running late. And my last patient was angry with me because the specialist we referred him to has a long waiting list. He shouted, jabbing his finger at me. I looked at him and thought, I'm just going to leave, I'm just going to walk out.

The paperwork is taking me twice as long as it normally does.

When I finish with the pathology reports, I go over them again, convinced that I've made a mistake in my distraction. I'm still hearing our phone call in my head. DI Tiernan told me that the man had bought the flask at a pawnshop in Dorset twenty years ago. So my father had never brought it out of the country, it was probably boxed up and sent with the rest of his belongings to my grandmother, and lost or picked up by someone along the way.

I wonder if the newspapers will learn about the sighting, and the thought exhausts me. Their ghoulishness, their relentless delight in the story.

It was domestic violence. There was nothing uncommon about it, nothing mysterious, except for his incompetence. A woman is murdered by her partner two times every week in this country. Eight a month, more than a hundred a year. No one would have cared about my father, no one would know his name, if he hadn't had money.

After finishing the forms, I turn off the lights and leave the practice. If he were innocent—if I didn't need to make a point— would I still be a doctor? I'm not like Laila or Rahul. Both of them have an intuition that I'm missing. Laila trained as a wilderness first responder when she was a teenager in Northumbria, Rahul became a paramedic while he was still at university. Neither of them has ever really considered doing anything else.

When I arrive home from work, I take Jasper to the canal. We stand in the dark, looking at the boats trapped in ice. I don't want to live here anymore.

After medical school, I was accepted by two hospitals for my foundation year. One was in London, the other in Edinburgh. We'd moved to Scotland after the murder, to Crail, a village on the east coast, and I'd done my degree at the University of Edinburgh. I had to decide whether to stay in Edinburgh, which I loved, or move to London, where, by living in the same city as my father's friends and the officers who'd investigated him, I might learn where he had gone.

I made the wrong choice. I should have stayed in Edinburgh. In different circumstances, I have a flat now in one of the terraces off Easter Road. I work as a journalist or an editor at an office in Merchiston. In the evenings, sometimes I go to the cinema and sometimes I meet my friends or my brother at a pizza restaurant by the Leith quays.

I've had these ideas since I was twelve. They're slightly pathetic, I know, and based on a few images seen on my first visit to Edinburgh. A bright open-plan office, a crowded restaurant, a woman standing under the canopy of a cinema.

London has such a hard polish, after Edinburgh. It's not crooked or mysterious. It doesn't have people silhouetted on the ridge of Arthur's Seat, or the sooty terraces, or the storms rolling in from the Firth of Forth. It doesn't have the same cheap, strip-lit fish shops with cursive neon signs, or the trattorias opened decades ago by Italian immigrants. It doesn't stay light until eleven in the summer, it's not close to the Highlands, it doesn't get as much snow. Though London never stood a chance, really. It reminds me of my father and Scotland of my mum.

9

M Y FATHER PUT DOWN his newspaper and asked Mum to go for a walk with him. They did two loops through St James's Park, then stopped to sit on a bench by the frozen pond. He said, "We don't have fun anymore."

Faye laughed. "What about last weekend?" A group of them had rented a villa in Mykonos, leaving their children at home with nannies or grandparents.

He shrugged.

"You seemed to enjoy yourself," she said. The villa had a pool, and scooters to ride into town, and a hammock, where he pulled her down to sleep next to him after they finished a bottle of ouzo.

He sighed. "We never do anything new," he said.

Sam had brought a few girls to Mykonos. On the first day, Sam stood by the deep end of the pool with an open bottle of champagne. The girls swam over to hold on to the ledge, and Sam said, "Open your mouths." The girls tilted back their heads. Sam poured the champagne into their mouths, a long white jet, then tipped the bottle so the champagne foamed onto their breasts.

"Like what?" asked Faye.

"Anything," he said.

"Is this about last night?" she asked. A senior partner at the bank had invited them for a kitchen supper at his house in Barnes, a long, dull night. He's just scared, thought Faye. He'll say, I don't want us to ever turn into that.

"No," he said. "The dinner was fine. I like Edward."

"Right."

Robbie was only five months old. That's what this is about, she thought, the responsibility of having a second child, the ordeal of his birth. Two days of labour, then her blood pressure dropped and they had to perform an emergency caesarean. She had been on the other side of the curtain, awake, while her body was temporarily disembowelled. No one had explained that part of it to her until afterwards. It had been difficult on Colin, too. He'd seen both sides of the curtain, he'd watched as she and the baby nearly died.

She was cold in the park, and wondered when they could go back inside. "Things will be easier by the spring," she said, and stamped her feet to warm them.

He looked at her then, and her legs went slack. Without the clatter of her boots on the ground, the air around them turned quiet. Her heart started to beat against her back.

"Do you love me?" she asked.

"Yes," he said, "but it's not how it used to be."

*

Near the end of the month, when he still hadn't come home, Faye sat in a chair with her eyes closed while a dentist worked in her mouth. Her jaw was numb, but she could still feel him tugging. Two of her wisdom teeth had become impacted and needed to be removed. She'd never even had a cavity before, but she was unsurprised. Her luck had run out.

Afterwards she walked down Belgrave Street with a raw, bleeding mouth. There were cotton pads in her bag, she'd need to switch the current one when the blood soaked through. The dentist had warned that her mouth would start to hurt as the anaesthetic wore off. Already she could feel twinges, thin wires of pain deep in her jaw.

The house would be empty when she got home, when she stood in the bathroom and changed the soaked cotton pads, when the feeling returned to her jaw and she tried to distract herself from the pain with an old film.

She'd always worried that he might meet someone else, but that would have been better. Colin hadn't fallen in love with another woman, as far as she knew, he'd just started to find her a bit boring.

She wanted to be alone so she could think of him. It was like the beginning, in that way. She looked forward to going to bed every night, so she could go over it without any interruptions.

A few weeks later, Rose opened her front door in a tailored shift and stockings. Her suitcase was behind her in the hall; she must have just got home. She'd been working on a case in Belfast for the past six weeks, and Faye had been waiting to talk to her about Colin in person. Faye breathed in the smell of her, like milled almond soap. She'd missed seeing her, they usually had dinner together at the pub by Cheyne Walk once a week.

"How was Ireland?"

"Fine," said Rose, which meant they'd won. Faye looked at Rose's clear, clever eyes. She was a good barrister, she understood why people behaved in certain ways, even when it went against their own best interests. She would understand why Colin had left, and once Faye knew that, she could fix it. "Want to go to the Cross Keys?" she asked.

Rose shook her head.

"Right, you must be tired from the trip, let's stay in. Shall I go pick up a bottle of wine?"

"I can't," said Rose.

Faye laughed. She looked at Rose's pale unpainted mouth, the sharp angle of her collarbone, which she'd broken in a riding accident. "You're not serious."

"I'm sorry," said Rose. "I've known him for longer."

10

I spent Christmas in Scotland with Nell. I'd invited Robbie, but he said he didn't fancy it. I tried not to think about how he would spend it instead. Nell lives in Crail now, she and her husband moved back after they had their son. We went for long walks on the coast path, and I told her about the man who had been arrested, who had not been my father.

"He's never going to be found," she said. She has been telling me this since we were sixteen. "You're only harming yourself."

My eyes smarted and I tried to argue with Nell, but she was right. It was so obvious there, on the coast path, with Rory ahead of us chasing Jasper, and the waves and the thick salt air. I wanted to be finished, I wanted to be clean of it.

For the past five months, I've been working, seeing my friends, going on dates, visiting Robbie at his flat in Peckham. I signed up for a boxing class, on Nell's suggestion, and a pottery one, on Laila's, and learned that I'm pretty good at boxing and terrible at pottery, though I love it. On the last bank holiday weekend, I went to Brighton with Laila and Harriet, and didn't think about my father at all. It's been a good spring, which is why, now, I'm trying not to think too much about what I'm doing.

The thing is, it came to me. It came into my flat, into my home. I'm on the mailing list for the Royal Court Theatre, and in the first week of April an invitation arrived to their spring benefit. I didn't look at it carefully at first, I might have recycled it without reading it at all, but then I was waiting for the kettle to boil, and the invitation was on the kitchen counter, and I picked it up. Inside was a list of the event's patrons, and the third one was James Fraser.

I went online and bought a ticket then, with the invitation still in my hand. I was worried it would already be sold out. The ticket was two hundred pounds, more than I usually spend in a week, but I typed in my credit card number and billing address. I did all of this automatically, like I hadn't even decided whether or not I'd go, and then I went back to the kitchen and finished making my tea.

It's the fifth of May now, and I'm across Sloane Square from the theatre, imagining what Nell would say if she knew. She would tell me to go home, she would ask if I want to go back to feeling the way I did for weeks after the sighting, dull and inert and defeated. A bus is coming up the King's Road. If I step forward, the driver will stop. I can leave now. But then I think of my father wrapping tape around a steel pipe, and I'm crossing the square to join the crowd outside the theatre doors.

I hold out my phone with the ticket and follow the others down the stairs, the noise growing louder until we're in a large room underground. I make it across the room to the bar, but I don't see James. I keep circling through the crowd as more people arrive and it grows harder to move. He might not come, I realize. He might only send a cheque.

Upstairs, the doors to a small black box theatre are open, and I sit down, staring at the empty, scratched stage, trying to work out what to do. If my father could see me now, I think he'd feel sorry for me, he'd find this pathetic. My head twitches, like that will clear away the thought. The first time I had it was in primary school in Crail, after I said something stupid in class and a few of the other children laughed—this idea of my father watching and being embarrassed for me—and I'm weary at still having it as an adult.

I leave to check the alley, even though James doesn't smoke, then try to find the men's toilets. I'm down a corridor, near the theatre's offices, when through an open door I hear voices and pots clinking.

A man comes out of the room holding a tray of lemon cakes, and I press my back to the wall so he can pass. I walk to the open door and look inside at a large industrial space under fluorescent lights. It might be used for costumes or storage normally, but now it's filled with long trestle tables covered in baking trays and tubs of ingredients. I can see red fruit inside one of the tubs, its liquid pressing against the plastic. Three people are working at different stations, two men and a woman, all moving at pace. I watch them absently, and then the woman at the middle table turns around, and the cords in the back of my neck stiffen.

I didn't know she was back. After university, Alice moved to San Francisco. She was still in America the last time I checked, she must have moved home recently. Her head is lowered, she doesn't see me crossing the room. She's bent from the waist, piping custard into a tray of éclairs with graceful, practised movements.

"Hello," I say, and she straightens. "I'm sorry to interrupt."

Alice smiles, waiting for me to continue. She looks the same. She never resembled her mum. Rose seems to belong indoors, and Alice outdoors. She has flushed cheeks, pale freckles, and dark blonde hair pulled back in a braid. Her teeth are white and still slightly crooked.

"I'm Claire." I've stopped breathing, I don't know what I'll say if she recognizes me.

"Alice," she says. We don't shake hands, she's still holding the piping bag. I imagine she's eager to finish the tray, but hiding her impatience. She's wearing a denim work shirt with a burlap apron tied over it. Her sleeves are rolled up, but she hasn't taken off her jewellery, a few thin gold bracelets and rings. Her polite expression doesn't shift with recognition. She's two years younger than me, she was only six the last time we saw each other, and my appearance has changed more than hers. Part of me is still disappointed, like there was a chance she'd be expecting me.

"The food's brilliant."

"Oh, thank you," she says, in a warm, slightly hoarse voice.

"Do you have a card?"

While she finds one for me, I remember, for the first time in years, the mirror at Ashdown with a frame made of white antlers. Alice and I used to dare each other to stand in front of it. It was strange to see your own reflection in the glass, like the mirror was meant to show you something else entirely.

11

AFTER THE SEPARATION, my father moved into a flat on Ebury Street. It was only around the corner, Mum always expected to see him in the neighbourhood, but the first time they ran into each other was two months later at a bar in Covent Garden, where a friend of Sabrina's was having a birthday party. "What are you doing here?" she asked.

"Sam's seeing Catherine," he said.

"Who's that?"

"Friend of Paula's. Why are you here?"

"She's Sabrina's mate from work."

Colin nodded. "What are you drinking?"

"Rum and Coke."

He smiled. "Of course you are." He turned to order, but kept his hand at the small of her back. The music was loud and he spoke with his mouth close to her head, so she could feel the warmth through her hair.

She made him laugh a few times, and he ducked his head, smiling. He was himself again. Not the strange, sardonic man who'd come to the house to fill boxes with his things. Who, when she asked what had made him suddenly decide to leave, had sighed and said, "No, I've known for a while."

"Come on," she said. "We should talk to other people."

"Why?" he asked.

My husband, she thought. They weren't even formally separated, he'd only been out of the house for two months.

They went on talking, and she went on saying the right thing, the funny or sharp or appealing thing. He was the warmest place in the world, and she lit up in return. She could be magnetic too, as it happened, she could marshal her own powers.

He said, "I don't get to do this anymore, I don't talk to anyone like this."

Faye considered him. She could leave, she could be in a cab in minutes, on her way home. One day, she wouldn't think about him every hour, her mind would be clear. She tried to make that the more appealing option.

He held her hand outside the bar, his other arm raised for a cab. She said, "Have you been with anyone else?"

"No," he said. "Have you?"

She shook her head. A cab drew up beside them. By the time they reached his flat, both of them were giddy, shushing each other on the stairs, pushing into the door as he turned the key, like they'd been kept apart against their will.

Afterwards she looked at herself in the mirror. Her pupils were large and black in the strange light, and she looked about nineteen. Colin put on a record. She tucked her legs beneath her on the sofa, and he kissed the top of her head.

At three in the morning, he toasted a baguette and put tiles of dark chocolate inside so they melted into the bread. It was her favourite snack, it had been since the trip to Perpignan when they stayed above a bakery, and he often made it for her. They ate standing in the kitchen, tearing at the bread, spilling the melted chocolate.

Faye woke first. When she put her feet on the cold floor, something was by her right foot, almost under the bed. She pulled the sheet out of the way and bent down to pick it up. A black hair tie, with a few blond hairs wrapped around it.

She went into the kitchen. The foil from the bread was still on the counter, the chocolate still dripped on the floor. She opened the dishwasher and saw two white cups and saucers, and two plates smeared with chocolate. Not theirs, though. Their plates were still in the sink. He'd made it for someone else.

Faye stayed in the kitchen until she heard Colin run a shower, then put on her clothes and waited for him to come out. "Are you free tonight?" she asked, out of perversity.

"I wish," he said, "but we have a client dinner." His voice wasn't pitching in the usual way, and he kept his eyes down as he towelled his hair.

"Right," she said. "I'm off."

He kissed her. His cheek was cold and wet from the shower, and he didn't meet her eyes. She went down the stairs. His car was parked in front of the building, and she stopped to consider it. She could put a brick through its windows. But that wouldn't cause enough damage, would it? Not nearly.

12

I STAY UP LATE after the Royal Court event searching for information about Alice. She has a catering business now; James must have recommended her for the event. I sift through her company's website, read an interview with her in a magazine, study pictures from a wedding she catered last week. Her social media accounts are private, but I can see that we have six friends in common. Four of my acquaintances from university, a consultant neurosurgeon I worked with at St George's, and Laila's cousin Reza.

Before our first patients arrive, I knock on the door to Laila's consulting room. "Do you want to get a drink tonight?"

"God no," she says, and points at the double espresso on her desk. "I'm shattered. Want to come over and watch something?"

After work, we pick up sushi on our way to her flat. While Laila changes into track leggings and a sweatshirt, she says, "They made me go to a club in Stoke Newington. I didn't get home until four."

It was her sister's birthday last night. "Did Yasmin have fun?" I ask, and Laila nods. We sit cross-legged on the couch and open the sushi boxes. She says, "Can we watch *Bake Off*?"

"That bad?"

"Yes." She finds the channel. "Look, they're doing pavlovas tonight."

"Do you know Alice Fraser?" I ask. Laila shakes her head. "She's friends with Reza."

"Oh, that Alice. Sure. She went out with Reza's friend. Why?"

"I saw her at a thing last night."

"What thing?"

"A fundraiser for the Royal Court."

"What were you doing at a fundraiser?"

"I like the Royal Court. Do you know her well?"

"No, this was ages ago, they were still in school. Is there any more wasabi?"

I hand her the container. "Do you think she'd recognize your name?"

Laila shrugs. "She'd recognize my surname from Reza."

"Can I follow her from your account?"

Laila doesn't set down the tub of miso soup in her hand. Without looking away from the screen, she says, "How do you know Alice?"

"Her parents were friends with my father," I say. Laila's mouth purses as she blows on the broth to cool it. I haven't told her anything about my father, except that he left us years ago and I don't know where he is now.

"How can Alice help?" she asks.

"I don't know yet," I say. "I think her parents might still talk to him."

Laila says, "Give me your phone." After a moment, she hands it back to me. She's downloaded the app, and typed in her username and password.

I thank her, and she waves her hand. "It's nothing. I never use it anyway." She spreads a blanket over us and says, "This part's going to be very tense. They can't burn the meringues."

When the episode ends, Alice still hasn't accepted the request. Laila stretches and says, "See you tomorrow," and then I'm on the night bus home, with her account open on my phone.

Alice might have overheard something. Her parents must have grown more relaxed about discussing it, especially in their own house. They might have even visited him. It's been decades, they're not under surveillance.

At home, I've taken Jasper for his night walk and changed for bed when my phone rings. "Claire Alden?" says a man. While he introduces himself, I move across the room, pick up a glass, put it down. The flat has grown smaller, unfamiliar, and I'm removed from it and numb.

"Your brother's had a seizure," says the doctor.

He's still alive. I never know how scared to be when I get calls like this, if someone would come to tell me the worst news in person. I close my eyes, still holding the phone to my ear, while the doctor asks if I need directions to the hospital, St Thomas' in Lambeth. I change into jeans and a sweatshirt, run down the stairs and out to Farringdon Road for a cab.

It's after midnight, there's no traffic. In sixteen minutes, we're crossing Blackfriars Bridge. "Which entrance?" asks the cab driver.

"A and E, please," I say, and my voice sounds distant, like water's blocking my ears.

I check in at A and E, and wait for my brother's doctor, who explains the circumstances of his seizure. Robbie collapsed outside a bus station. A witness called an ambulance. He had a generalized tonic-clonic seizure.

"Have you done an ECG?"

The doctor nods. "It was normal."

"How long was he unconscious?"

"Three minutes."

I wince. I can't stop picturing him convulsing. Someone was with him, at least. The witness stayed with him until the ambulance came, she was holding his hand when the paramedics arrived.

"Have you asked him about going into a detox?"

"He hasn't agreed to that yet," says the doctor.

When I find his room, my brother is sitting up in bed. He's thin enough for me to see the tendons in his neck. "Hi, Robbie."

"Hey."

I hug him, kiss the side of his head. "Are you sore?"

"A little," he says. We won't talk about the detox tonight. He needs to rest. He's been given a tranquillizer to help with the withdrawal, but he's still sweating, and he's been scratching his arm since I came into the room.

He moves over so that I can sit on the bed next to him, and we watch a singing competition show. Robbie makes jokes about the performance. He's still funny, still a good mimic. Everything to him—his kindness, gentleness, intelligence—is still here, but the tramadol has changed how he looks and sounds. He doesn't smell like himself anymore.

When the show ends, I stand to go. "Are you comfortable? Do you need more water?"

"I'm fine."

"I'll come tomorrow morning. Are you sure you have everything you need?"

He nods. "They brought my bag." A red backpack is next to his bed, within arm's reach.

I ride down in the lift. I wait for the night bus. I open the door to my flat, to my warm bed, my stocked fridge, my job and friends and appointments. I think of my brother trying to fall asleep in the hospital with one arm around his backpack.

Three years ago, when he was twenty-four, Robbie called me at work and said, "I think I've done something to my knee."

He'd been playing five-a-side football when his leg twisted.

"Does it hurt?"

"Um," he said. "It's not good," which meant it was excruciating.

"You have to go to A and E."

"I have a seminar tonight." He was in a postdoctoral program at Bristol University, studying mechanical engineering. He wanted to design robotics for prosthetic limbs.

"You can make up the work."

I drove over to Bristol that night. He'd torn a cruciate ligament in his right knee and would need surgery. The earliest surgery appointment was in six days. I remember standing in his bathroom, brushing my teeth, and saying, "What have they given you for the pain?"

"Tramadol," he said.

I asked him to show me the box. His doctor had prescribed fifty milligrams a day. It's an opioid painkiller, like codeine or fentanyl, and as addictive. I asked Robbie if he'd read the safety information, if he understood the risks, then—and this is the part I'll never understand, or forgive myself for—I handed him back the box.

It should be simple. He was prescribed the medication for pain, he's not in pain anymore, he should be able to stop taking it.

He's tried. When he stops taking tramadol, he has withdrawal. His ears start to ring, and the ringing gets louder and louder. He has pins and needles in his legs and arms. He can't sleep. He has nausea, like motion sickness, which doesn't get better even after he vomits until he's spitting up bile. He becomes dizzy, his nose runs, his skin sweats. A persistent voice in his ear says that, actually, he's not a good person, that he's pathetic, and he doesn't want to listen, but he's tired.

He's tried to quit four times, that I know of. There have probably been more. I've made appointments for him at detoxes and rehabs, and he's come close, but every time he baulks.

I can't believe now how casual both of us were at his house in Bristol the night of his injury. Robbie, I remember, was disappointed about not being able to play football in the summer, and I was worried about asking for the days off work to help after his surgery. We chatted, started the dishwasher, and went to sleep, while the box of tramadol sat on his kitchen counter.

I should have known. He'd never been very good to himself. He'd forget to eat, stay up all night studying, not use his inhaler even when his asthma made it hard to breathe.

Robbie looks like our father. Sometimes I wonder if that's why he mistreats himself. It's the only act of revenge he can take.

It's been three years. He buys tramadol online now, and he's at six hundred milligrams a day. He'll have more seizures if he doesn't stop, or it will be something worse.

I bought him a naloxone auto-injector last year. If he overdoses, he has to hold the auto-injector against his thigh and press down, and the naloxone will keep his airways from collapsing. I carry one too, even though the chances are so small that I'll be there when he overdoses.

When I return to the hospital in the morning, Robbie is in bed, drinking juice from a cup with a foil lid.

"I brought some books." He likes graphic novels, he has since he was little. I asked the assistant at the bookshop for recommendations.

"Thanks," he says, sifting through them. "Oh, I wanted to read this one. It had good reviews."

I look at his leg under the blanket. He's done physical therapy for his knee, it's healed properly. He can walk and run without trouble from it. This injury should have barely affected his life.

"They want you to stay for seventy-two hours."

"I know," he says. I hand him the pamphlet for Penbridge and wait as he opens it. This one's a twenty-eight-day programme in an old brick house in Oxfordshire. It has a large garden, and good meals. I know those things don't really matter with this, but maybe they will help convince him.

"Will you think about it?"

"Yes."

My brother was only fourteen months old at the time of the murder. He didn't remember any of it; we told him when he turned sixteen. I think that must be worse. He's so angry. We both are, but you can see it in him more.

13

ALICE ACCEPTED the request while I was visiting Robbie. She doesn't post often, maybe once or twice a week, but she's had the account for four years. I don't know how to record all the information, the contents of the pictures, the locations, her captions, the comments, her replies. I open a spreadsheet, label different columns, and start to fill them in. Soon a dozen rows are full, and I've only gone through her first two weeks of pictures.

Alice was twenty-eight when she opened the account. She was still living in San Francisco and working at a restaurant in the Presidio. Most of her pictures then were taken outdoors, on hikes and camping trips in Big Sur, Point Reyes, Bolinas. There's a picture of her swimming in Mirror Lake in Yosemite. The next one shows her friend—her closest, I think, a woman named Amelia—on the far side of a campfire. Then the same friend at a wedding. Alice is invited to a lot of weddings. One in Cumbria, one in Provence, one at Ashdown for her cousin.

Her picture from Ashdown shows lambs grazing on the lawn behind the ceremony. All of the lambs are wearing green wreaths, which someone made and slipped onto them for the wedding. What a completely mad use of money, though it does look nice.

Two years ago, she posted a picture of a man named Matthew in ski boots and a thermal shirt. He's in her pictures often from then on. She posted one of them at a night market in Hong Kong. It must have been hot, she's wearing a short white dress and sandals, smiling at him with his arm around her shoulders. There's a picture of him on a sofa a few months later, with a Christmas tree behind him and piles of wrapping paper on the floor. I can't see much else, but enough to know that it's the drawing room at Ashdown. In the last picture of him, he's holding a bottle of sherry with a handwritten tag that says, "Drink me."

Alice moved back to England about a year ago. She posted a picture of her new keys, and of the Chinese food she ordered while unpacking, but nothing about why she moved or why Matthew didn't come with her. She started the catering company soon after returning to London, and began posting more pictures of food. Langoustines and butter, linguine alle vongole, a cauldron of paella. A wooden table in a meadow with a laptop, a notebook, and a slice of olive-oil cake. "My office," says the caption. She's done this before, she posted a picture from southern France of her computer, a glass of rosé, and a silver tray of ice and oysters. The caption said, "Working lunch."

Her friend Amelia appears rarely after the move, though there's a picture of her baby, Alice's godson, in a striped romper, with closed, wrinkled eyes and a tiny snub nose.

Last summer, Alice posted a photo of two of her friends on the terrace at Ashdown, in leggings and jumpers, with cups of tea and newspapers around them. They all look like they've just woken up. I study the picture and my pulse speeds. She invites friends to her parents' house, then.

At four, I take a break to walk Jasper. I turn onto the main road. Piles of rubbish spill out of the bins, and flyers for a delivery service are scattered on the doorsteps or trodden into the ground. There's a flattened takeaway carton in the road, and a chicken bone with a bit of gristle.

When I see my reflection in a pub window, I think, Look at the state of you. My raincoat is bunched over my jumper, my jeans are too tight, my hair is frizzing in the rain. I try to straighten my coat and hair. I walk past the people under the pub awning without meeting any of their eyes.

I know what Alice would photograph here—the row of old wrought-iron streetlamps on Clerkenwell Green. She probably wouldn't post it, though.

We keep walking for almost an hour in the drizzle, and slowly the effect wears off. It's like coming out of the cinema in the afternoon.

On Sunday morning, I go back to the hospital to see Robbie. He looks better, though he didn't have a good night, even with the sleep medication they gave him. Every so often, a tremor runs down his face. This is the longest he's gone without tramadol for months.

We talk, watch an Arsenal match, play cards. I want to tell him about Alice, about this plan that's taking shape, but it would be selfish, it's not what he should be thinking about now. He's agreed to go into Penbridge after the seventy-two hours. This might be almost over, he might be almost through.

The founder of one of the companies that sells tramadol has a mansion in Maida Vale. Last spring, the mother of a boy in Northern Ireland who died of a tramadol overdose sat outside his mansion for three weeks in protest. I took her a flask of tea and sandwiches, though she said she didn't need them, people had been bringing her more cooked meals than she could eat.

I send Alice an email on Monday morning after rewriting it in my head a dozen times over the weekend. I say that we met at the Royal Court event and ask if she would be available to cater a party at the end of the summer for my parents' anniversary.

I don't have any time between patients to check my phone until two. Alice has answered, a short, polite reply that thanks me for my note and asks if we can speak on the phone about my event. I send back times, then write, "Or I can come by your office?"

"We don't have an office yet," she says. "I do all the recipe testing from home. I'm in Chelsea, would that work for you?"

We agree on Thursday at seven thirty, and she gives me her home address.

After work, I buy a tin of black shoe polish and listen to the radio while cleaning my boots. There's one picture from Alice's account that I keep thinking about. I don't know why it makes me so angry, it's no worse than any of the others.

It shows a bathtub at Ashdown with a wooden board across it. There's a thick novel on the board and a cup of green tea. The bath faces a window with its shutters pulled back. Outside is a long view of a winter afternoon, with scratched trees and dark clouds. You can just make out a few sheep on the lawn. She must have taken the picture from the bath, though you can't see her body. "How long are you there?" a friend asked, and Alice wrote, "Just down for the day."

Not angry, exactly. Jealous. She can see her mum whenever she wants.

14

MUM WAS WAITING for me at the school gates, with Robbie in his pram. She was wearing a wool coat and stockings. The pram was a Silver Cross, lofted and heavy and "completely idiotic," Mum often said, "in a city." After we turned onto our road, Robbie started crying, and she said, "Almost there." I walked beside them in my uniform, a navy skirt and blazer, down the row of tall white houses with black numbers.

Mum lifted Robbie and hurried up our steps. She set him down in the front hall, wailing, and I crouched next to him until she came back into view, bumping the pram up the steps. Once the door was closed, she smashed the pram into the wall. Not for the first time, there were dents in the plaster all along the front hall.

Mum carried Robbie upstairs, and I went down to the kitchen to find Emma. "Hello," she said, and gave me a kiss. "Do you want to help me cook?"

Emma was our nanny, though she looked enough like Mum that most people assumed she was our aunt, which I liked.

"I'm making a tarte tatin," said Emma. She was wearing a navy pinafore with a white shirt underneath. The pinafore was hers and the shirt Mum's.

Emma often borrowed Mum's clothes and cassettes. She helped herself to the wine in the cellar and the books on the shelves and the contents of the fridge. Whenever she asked, Mum shrugged and said, "Go ahead. I didn't pay for it." She seemed to like the idea of her and Emma scavenging the contents of the house, which had been paid for by my father, or my grandmother.

Emma had arrived nine months before, soon after our father left, and they'd become very close in that time. "Living under one roof," said Mum, "is an accelerant." "Like university," said Emma, and Mum agreed, though neither of them had been.

They fought often, shouting up the stairs, sighing loudly, muttering, "She's being impossible," and they often laughed so hard they had to hold on to the kitchen counter, wheezing, their eyes streaming.

Emma cooked and Mum cleaned. They took turns taking out the bins. Emma was better than Mum at getting Robbie down for a nap, but he still reached for Mum whenever she came into a room, or followed her with his eyes.

During the week, when she wasn't watching us, Emma went to auditions and rehearsals and sometimes bought rush tickets for shows. Her favourite writer was Caryl Churchill, she'd seen *Fen* twelve times at the Almeida. She left bound scripts around the house, and sometimes read parts of them aloud to me.

That night, Emma was waiting to hear about an audition. She

always cooked a lot when she was waiting. The producers were deciding between her and one other actress, and would announce their decision by the end of the week.

"They certainly take their time, don't they?" said Emma. I nodded. She sighed and wiped the back of her hand over her forehead, mussing her hair. Her eyes were hazel with a black ring around the iris.

She'd spent weeks before the audition on the character's accent. She always prepared a lot for every role, and had learned to play the piano for one character. "Do you have to play piano onstage?" asked Mum.

"No," said Emma. "It's for me. I'm building behind the role."

At the far end of the room, glass doors opened onto the rear garden and the dull grey sky. I stood with my face to the cold glass. Someone moved past the gate in the rear wall. It faced onto an alley, which was usually empty. I watched for a while, but there was no more movement.

"Can you wash the apples for the tart?" asked Emma, and I moved to the sink. I set the dripping apples on the cutting board and Emma sliced them with a weighted carving knife. Soon Mum came downstairs with Robbie and strapped him into his high chair. He twisted under the straps and jerked his head from side to side as she tried to spoon baby food into his mouth. She gave him pasta, which he threw to the floor, then some banana. He began crying, his small, fat body leaning over the shelf, mashing his hands in the banana. Mum said, "Right," and lifted him from the high chair to carry him back upstairs. A few minutes later, we heard water thudding into the bath.

I ran a tea towel under the tap and wiped down the high chair.

While the pastry cooled in the fridge, Emma heated the chicken soup she'd made earlier. As the pot warmed, the kitchen filled with the smell of broth. We ate at the long oak refectory table. It could fit eight people, though it never did, not since our father had moved out.

He lived in a flat a few minutes' walk away, and we saw him on the weekends. Mum always left the house before he arrived to collect us. Sometimes she asked me what we'd done or talked about, and listened with a calm face and her nails working at the skin around her thumbs.

Mum came back downstairs in a dress patched with wet, and Emma pointed at the pot on the hob. "There's some left," she said. Mum said, "Thanks," but she didn't serve herself any, or join us at the table. She filled a glass with white wine and carried it outside. The garden was dark, but I could see her by the light from the kitchen, standing with her arms around herself. Our spoons clinked against the bowls while Emma and I talked about my school's winter concert, and a friend of hers who was shooting a short film in Battersea Park over the weekend, and if we should go watch. We heard crying from the nursery, and then it stopped. "He must be worn out," said Emma. She blew out the candle and a crooked ladder of smoke rose from the wick.

While the tarte tatin cooked, I did my homework and Emma read *The Birthday Party* with her stockinged feet crossed on the table. The bottoms of the stockings were dusty, their soles grey. She had left the oven light on, and inside the metal rack and scorched wall glowed. Next to us the egg timer clicked down. When the timer sounded, Emma put on a Nick Cave record and we ate the tart while he sang.

Daisy hopped down the stairs. She had been a gift from my father, a Netherland dwarf rabbit, white with brown spots. The day before, Emma had come up from the garden with the rabbit cradled against her chest. Someone had left the gate open, she'd been in the alley. Daisy stood on her hind legs with her small front paws folded at her chest, her whiskers twitching. I put a drop of vanilla extract on my finger and she licked it off.

"It's starting," Mum called down, and we went upstairs to watch *House of Eliott*. I leaned against Mum on the sofa. When she yawned, her ribs expanded into me. She put her arm around me, bracelets clinking, and I slid down against her. With my ear to her chest, I listened to her swallow and clear her throat. She smelled like white wine and oranges.

I lay with my head on Mum's lap and she smoothed my hair. On screen, Charles followed Bea onto the hotel roof. Mum's hand stalled, then started up again.

Two hours later, Emma was reading a script at the kitchen counter. Everyone else had gone to bed, and the room was dim, the only light coming from a pendant lamp. A man came into the room. He was wearing gloves and holding a steel pipe.

When Emma saw him, she reached across the counter for the heavy carving knife on the draining rack. It was just beyond her grasp. She tried to pull the draining rack closer, but it tilted and crashed to the floor on the far side of the counter, the knife skittering out of reach.

He brought the pipe down on her head, and her legs buckled. She kicked and clawed at him, pushing him back until she wasn't pinned against the counter anymore. The door to the garden was still open behind them, and she struggled against him. The floor grew slick under her feet. She almost made it to the door. Then she was fighting in place, trying to block the blows. He hit her again, and she kept fighting him even as her skull began to flood.

When Mum heard the sounds from the basement, she came down from her room and met him on the landing. She tried to run past him to the front door, but he grabbed her arm and scraped the sharp edge of the pipe across her chest. She shoved him away, but he cracked her head against the wall. When she came to, he was holding her up against the wall and punching her.

He reached his hand down her throat. She couldn't breathe, his hand was choking her. She drove her knee between his legs, and he jerked backwards.

She stumbled through the door, onto the road, and ran to the Blacksmith's Arms. She stood on the threshold in her dress and stockinged feet, washed in blood, and said, "Help me."

Upstairs, in my bedroom, I heard a rasping, tearing sound. Like someone trying to breathe. I thought I was imagining it at first. Then there was a thud, hard enough to shake the wall in my room, and the sound stopped. I closed my eyes, but my body was trembling under the blanket.

I went to Mum's room first, but her bed was empty, the covers drawn back. I climbed down the stairs in the dark. The front door was open and cold air was blowing into the house. My teeth started to chatter.

Mum wouldn't have left the door open. I thought I should close it, in case someone was outside, but couldn't bring myself to go near it. There was something wet by the door. I couldn't see it clearly in the dark, but it was moving, dripping down the wall.

The skin all across my body was jumping with my pulse. I made it down to the kitchen. A faint circle of light from the pendant lamp shone on Emma's script and glass of red wine, and everything was still and quiet.

Someone had knocked over the draining rack, and one of the knives lay near my feet. There was a terrible, rusty smell in the room. I moved around the counter. Emma was lying on her back, with her arm bent towards her face. The room was dark, but I could see that her head was wet.

I crawled to her side. The floor was slippery under my hands and knees. I started to push the wet hair from her face, but my fingers were thick and clumsy. I bent close to her, until I could see the red wine stains in the grooves in her mouth. She smelled like sandalwood.

When I heard voices, I thought the people who hurt Emma had come back, and I ran into the other room to hide. I crawled behind a chair and stared at its fabric with both of my hands over my mouth. Someone at the top of the stairs switched on the lights in the basement, and I covered my head in my arms.

A man was bending down to pick me up. I kept making the same keening sound, and he said, "It's all right, love, you're safe, you're safe." He lifted me and my arms went around his neck, my mouth gaping against his coat. He told me to close my eyes. He said, "I'll count down from ten for you."

But I opened them too early, and over his shoulder I saw Emma lying on her back, under the lights. There was chipped gold varnish on her nails and a faint stamp on the back of her hand from the concert she'd been to the night before. There was red on the floor around her, and it was on me too, my legs and arms and nightdress were stained.

In the morning, an officer found my father's car seventy miles south of London, abandoned in a field above the Channel. One of its doors was hanging open, and there were stains on the front seat, as though the driver had been head to toe in blood.

PART TWO

FOREIGN

15

THE SEARCH BEGAN in the field by the Channel where his car was found. Soon there were dozens of police officers spread across it. The police didn't know if any of the blood in the car was his, if he had been injured in the attack, if he had crawled somewhere nearby to hide.

The edge of the field was a cliff, with a sheer drop to the water. A Zodiac with police divers was sent from around the headland. There was a chance he had jumped. They'd found his wallet in the car, with cash inside. He hadn't tried to clean the bloodstains from the seat and he'd left the car in a field within clear view of the village, where it would be easily found.

If he hadn't jumped, he might have walked down to the village, Newhaven, and boarded a ferry across the Channel to France. He might have left his car by the cliff deliberately, to make it look like a suicide. By the time the car was found, the first two crossings had already left. Officers interviewed everyone at the port, and detectives in France waited at Dieppe to search the ferries when they arrived.

The search spread across Newhaven. Officers knocked on doors and climbed into attics and searched the row of painted beach huts. The town curved around a harbour, and on the docks officers searched under tangles of nets and buoys for stains or footprints. Everyone who owned a boat in Newhaven was ordered to check if it had been stolen. My father had experience with boats, he'd grown up sailing on the Norfolk Broads.

A hundred army reservists joined the search. The police had been granted more resources than usual. They didn't want to make a mistake, with the story leading every newspaper in the country.

The soldiers and officers spread from Newhaven onto the South Downs, where they needed scythes to cut through the gorse. They kept searching overnight while the rain turned to sleet.

On the second day of the search, a motorboat was reported missing. It was a small wooden boat, white with a green stripe. A local man owned six of them to rent to tourists, and now there were five.

The boat had an outboard engine and a rudder. It was meant for short trips, but could in theory make it across the Channel. The owner didn't know when the boat had gone missing, since he hadn't rented any of them out since August. There had been a strong storm a few weeks before, the boat might have been torn from its moorings.

It looked like the boat my father and Mum rented in Positano years before. They went out on it with a bottle of wine and grissini. They'd told me the story, about how my father fell asleep, how they hadn't realized there was a strong current, how the boat floated so far from shore that they didn't make it back until after dark. I think he'd been drunk, though they left that part out. It would have happened faster than usual, he'd been in the sun all day. Mum could have got something around his neck then, if she'd known. Instead of lying next to him on the boat's bench, lifting his heavy arm and putting it around herself, and letting the boat drift further from the coast.

———

A STRANGE THING happens when I read about the search. It seems to have nothing to do with those first days afterwards in London, or with what had happened inside our house, or with me now.

The search seems staged. I look at a picture of officers in a field, and I can't believe they ever expected to find him.

Six years ago, I drove to Newhaven. I crossed the field where his car was found and looked over the edge of the cliff. There were a lot of rocks, you'd have to be careful to avoid them if you wanted to land in the water. But I know he didn't jump. His friends wouldn't have risked so much to protect him unless they knew he was alive.

16

THE FIRST DAYS afterwards were quiet and muffled for me. It was raining. I couldn't eat, and I slept a lot. Mum was still in hospital, and we were staying with Sabrina at her flat in Edgware. I don't remember leaving the flat. Sabrina read to me, and we played with Robbie. I had no idea what was happening at the same time. This huge, frantic search. Sabrina kept me away from the news, though I don't remember being curious. I didn't know then that my father was a suspect. I thought it had been burglars.

While the police were searching the Downs for my father, Sabrina was folding my hands in a warm towel. She wiped my palms, between my fingers. I expected the towel to be stained red and brown when she finished, but there was nothing on me, she had put me into the shower the night before as soon as we got to her flat.

Sabrina rubbed my knuckles and the webbing between each finger, then filled a bowl with pebbles and warm water. "What are the pebbles for?" I asked.

"No idea," she said. When I stirred my fingers, the pebbles clinked. It was a good sound, like the shingle clattering on a beach, and I did it again.

She'd made a nest for me with quilts and a velveteen bear on one side of her bed. Sometime in the night, I had screamed hard enough to burst the blood vessels above my eye, leaving a row of bright red dots.

Sabrina shook a bottle of coral varnish. She worked carefully, dragging the brush over each nail. The scent of the varnish filled my nose, burning away the smells from the night before.

My nails were still wet when Sabrina drove me to the hospital to visit Mum. A nurse led us down the corridor and into a room where Mum was spitting blood into a cup. When she saw us, she wiped the red mess from her mouth with the back of her hand. I didn't move from the doorway. Sabrina was already next to Mum, kissing her, taking the dirty cup, asking the nurse for some water.

Mum looked past Sabrina at me, hopefully at first, then her face sagged as she realized that I was afraid of her. There was still red around her mouth, and Sabrina handed her a tissue. I stepped closer. Her cheeks were bruised and swollen, like apples had been pushed underneath them. She was trying to angle part of her head away from me, but I could see where her blond hair had been shaved and her scalp punched with black stitches. Her hospital gown was thin enough to show the gauze bandages on her chest and stomach. She touched her hand to one of the bandages, like something was happening underneath it, or it was hurting her.

I sat next to her on the bed and she took my hand, even though two of her fingers were in splints. She said, "I'm so sorry. I know it's not easy to see me like this, but there's something I have to tell you." She was speaking slowly, trying not to slur the words. She said, "Your father was angry with me. He wasn't angry with you."

I didn't understand why she was telling me this. I hadn't thought he was angry with me, though I was furious with him. He shouldn't have moved into the flat on Ebury Street, he should have been there to help Mum and Emma fight them.

"He loved you very much," she said, then stopped, and stared down at her lap. She was having trouble breathing. Behind her, Sabrina was crying, with her face lifted and her eyes closed. "Your father hurt me and Emma."

"Did they make him?" I asked.

"Who?"

"The burglars."

"No. There weren't any burglars. No one came into the house except him."

I nodded, but only to make her stop. I didn't believe her.

The next day, while Sabrina gave Robbie a bath, I called my grandmother. Someone else answered—one of her staff—and I waited, staring at the door, listening for water draining from the tub.

"Where's Dad?" I asked when she came on the line.

"We don't know," said my grandmother. Her voice sounded even more brittle on the phone.

"Mum said he hurt her."

"She's confused. Anyone could be under those conditions," she said. "Your father was walking past the house and saw a fight in the basement. He went inside to stop it and the man ran off."

I wasn't relieved, exactly, I'd known that Mum was wrong.

"He's going away to collect his thoughts," she said. "He'll be back soon, and all of this will be straightened out." She knew this because he'd sent her a letter, she said.

"Did he send a letter for me?" I asked.

"I don't know," said my grandmother. "Where are you?"

I looked through the window and tried to think of a lie. "Sabrina's flat."

My grandmother sighed. "You should be with family." It had been wrong of me to call her, and now this would be my punishment, the cold house in Norfolk. "I'd like to speak to Sabrina."

In the bathroom, Sabrina lifted Robbie into a towel and took the phone from me, cradling him against her with one arm. "Hi, Deborah," she said. She glanced at me and I looked at the floor, ashamed. "Hmm," said Sabrina. "No, Faye wants the children to stay here." She moved into the sitting room, but I could still hear her. "Would you like to come and visit them?" she asked. There was a long pause, then she said, "I think while Faye's in hospital, it would be best not to involve lawyers, don't you?"

After the call ended, Sabrina went into the kitchen and began beating a packet of frozen strawberries against the counter.

"I'm sorry," I said.

"That's all right, she's your grandmother, you're allowed to call her." Sabrina dropped a handful of strawberries into the blender and poured in milk. "Do you want honey?" When I didn't answer, she said, "Sweetheart, you have to try to eat something."

"Dad sent her a letter." It seemed to take Sabrina a long time to cross the room and come to stand in front of me. "It's a mistake. Mum thinks it's him, but it wasn't."

She went still. "Where did he send the letter from?"

MY GRANDMOTHER had already taken the letter to the police by the time she told me. My father probably included instructions asking her to turn it in as his defence. The letter was postmarked from Sussex, from the village where Rose and James Fraser live.

In his memoir, the lead detective described asking Rose, "Did Colin Spenser come to your house on the eighteenth of November?"

"Yes," she said.

"Why didn't you tell us?"

"It didn't seem relevant," said Rose.

She had been alone in the house that night. James was working in London, and Alice was away at boarding school. As she told it, she was surprised to see my father's car at the gate. He was in shock, said Rose, and almost incoherent.

He told her he'd seen something through the window and went inside to help. The attacker ran away, but Mum was badly hurt, and confused, and accused him of trying to kill her.

"Why didn't he call the police?" asked the detective.

Rose said, "He panicked. He thought they wouldn't believe him, if it was her word against his. She can make herself very sympathetic."

When the detective mentioned the stains in Colin's car, Rose said yes, there was blood on his clothes when he arrived at her house. He'd tried to resuscitate Emma, there had been a lot of blood, he was barely aware it was on him. She gave him some brandy for the shock, and he promised to call the police in the morning and explain. She said he went upstairs to bed, but when she woke in the morning he was gone.

Rose is a barrister. She must have planned every word to protect herself from being charged with obstruction.

The police descended on Ashdown. I've seen aerial photographs of their search, the drive so full of vehicles that some were parked on the grass. Dozens of officers in white forensic suits searched the terrace and the lawn on their hands and knees. More were down by the stables, and two officers were rolling back the cover on the swimming pool. And there was one, standing inside the walled garden, ghostly in his pale boilersuit. He looked strange in there, away from the others, as though he'd got lost.

It had been forty-eight hours since the murder. The police now believed that my father had never been in Newhaven, that one of his friends had left his car in the field as a decoy, that searching it and the South Downs had been pointless. Rose denied that she'd driven my father's car to Newhaven. The detective asked, "Where did Lord Spenser go when he left your house?"

"I don't know," she said. "But I expect he'll be back soon."

Two detectives separated the household staff and began interviews inside one of the vans parked on the grass. They brought photographs. The first was of Emma on the Pont Marie, sitting on the bridge wall in a jumper and rolled-up jeans. Behind her was a hotel on the Île Saint-Louis with small yellow awnings over every window. Her hair was loose around her shoulders, and her eyes were warm and bright.

In the second she was on her back with wet hair scraped away from her face. She had bruises on her shoulders where my father had held her in place and a red mark on her mouth where he'd slapped her. Some of the staff cried, but none of them admitted to seeing him.

The next day, while officers continued to search the house, Rose maintained her Sunday routine. She went for a hack in the woods behind the property, and spent a while cleaning her horse. She had a bath. Neither she nor James had been arrested, they would still eat at home that night, at the table in the kitchen, as they always did on Sundays.

From our visits, I remember the dinners Rose requested for the end of the weekend. A shepherd's pie, fish cakes, a roast leg of lamb. The sort of food she considered simple, even though it took hours to prepare. They ate in the warm kitchen, with the curtains drawn so they didn't have to see the police torches outside.

17

"I'LL PICK YOU up at seven," I tell Robbie, trying to work out how to get from the practice to St Thomas' in time. "We'll get to Penbridge around eight thirty, they said that's fine."

"I talked to my boss," says Robbie.

He works as an insurance adjuster. The firm sends him in after a storm, flood or fire to assess the damage and decide how much the homeowners should be paid. I think he does this work not because he likes it, but so that someone less sympathetic, who might try to save money for the insurance firm, won't. He was hired last winter after the floods in Yorkshire. There was a short interview and training process, the firm was desperate for assessors. He usually works for a few months at a time, then has a long break before the next assignment.

"Good," I say. "It was probably best to let him know you'll be out of touch this month."

"They want me to go up to Lancashire."

"No."

"It'll be good, it'll be a change of scene."

"Robbie, just try a night at Penbridge, you can leave if you want."

"I need this job."

"They won't fire you for taking medical leave. You don't have to tell them why."

"I can't. Bye, Claire."

I call Robbie's mobile, which he's switched off, then the hospital. A receptionist connects me to his unit, and another one puts me on hold. I stare at the clock on the wall of my consulting room. Six minutes on hold, then nine. She says, "Sorry for the wait. How can I help?"

"Can I speak to Robbie Alden, please? This is his sister."

She sets the phone down. I wait, tapping my pen on the desk. The nurse says, "He's just discharged himself."

I fold in half, staring at the carpet, my arms wrapped around my waist. I think of Robbie at the hospital yesterday, reading intently, as he has since he was little, a shock of hair falling over his forehead. I try to remember it clearly, in case it's the last time I'll see him.

———

FOR MONTHS AFTER the murder, every morning when I left for school, I expected to see my father on the other side of the road. I expected him to hold his finger to his mouth, telling me to be quiet, and for us to walk down the road into the park. He'd look different. A rougher coat. A beard. Thinner. He would say, There's been a terrible mistake. He would call me by my old name. My father always said my name differently to anyone else. He made it sound like a longer word, or a more significant one, as though it had more syllables.

It took me a long time to stop loving him. I worry that a part of me still does, and that I only want to find him to say that I'm not angry, that he doesn't have to stay away.

I see him standing in the shallows off the coast of Dorset, tightening the strap on a snorkel mask before handing it to me and saying, "Try it now, does that fit?"

Him holding up two scarves at a stall in a Christmas market. "Right, which would your mum like?"

Mum answering the phone and laughing, her hand pressed to her chest, saying, "Oh, thank god, I thought you'd had an accident."

Him holding Robbie in our garden and pointing up at a line of migrating geese.

All of it happened, and yet it somehow ended here. A few months before he injured his knee, before he took tramadol for the first time, Robbie turned to me on the tube and said, "Are you tired of thinking about him? I'm so tired of thinking about him."

———

I CROSS ONTO Alice's street on Thursday in a warm spring twilight. She lives in Chelsea, near the border of Fulham. I've never been here before. The sky is marbled with pink clouds, and there's so much of it, since all the buildings are low enough to leave an open view. Under the clouds are rows of houses with glossy front doors, two churches, and a pub with wicker chairs out the front. The houses, which are square with flat roofs and painted trims, seem ordinary and achievable, except they're in Chelsea, so are neither.

I ring her bell, then straighten my clothes and hair. I'm wearing jeans, ankle boots, and a new slate-grey cashmere jumper purchased for the occasion. A bee comes to hover around me, and I'm brushing it away when the bolts slide back and the door creaks on its hinges. Alice is wearing a striped shirt and jeans cuffed above her bare feet.

"Hello," she says, as a small shepherd dog sniffs my legs. "This is Stella. Sorry, I forgot to ask if you're all right with dogs."

"Of course. She must smell mine," I say, as people always do. I follow Alice down the hall to the kitchen, which has large windows, polished counters, and an old-fashioned oven with brass dials.

"Would you like some tea? Coffee?"

"Tea, thanks." Alice fills a kettle and sets it to boil. I recognize the oven from the picture she posted on Sunday of a roast chicken with charred lemons.

"Did you enjoy the event last week?" she asks.

I nod. "It's my favourite theatre."

"Mine too. Did you see *Hangmen*?"

"I loved it." While she reaches onto a shelf for two mugs, we talk about the play. I tell her that it struck me so much that I walked the four miles home after seeing it, which is true, and Alice says she went back the next night for a second performance.

She screws the lids on a few jars of flour and sugar. "Sorry for the mess."

"Not at all." On the counter are stone mixing bowls, with open shelves stacked with glasses and plates above them. Every bit of the kitchen is artful, even the washing-up liquid. The brass dials on the oven are spoked, like a ship's wheel. It's so different from my flat, and my friends'. No stained takeaway menus, or half-eaten Mars bars, and I doubt she shoved any into the drawers just before I arrived.

She clears a space for us at the dining table, pushing aside a laptop and appointment diary, and flips to a clean page in a notebook. "So, tell me about your event."

"It's my parents' anniversary."

"Oh, yes, you said. How long have they been married?"

"Forty years. The party's going to be a surprise." Our accents are similar; I tried to change mine when we moved north, but couldn't entirely.

She asks me about the date and the venue. While she takes down notes, I look out at the flowers and herbs in the garden. We could be in the countryside. A tennis racquet leans against the fence, and a fringed cotton hammock is strung between two trees. I think it's the one she bought on a trip to Hydra.

The doorbell rings, and Stella barks at the sound. She's a gorgeous dog, like a miniature husky, with patches of cream and grey fur and different-coloured eyes. "Just a minute," says Alice.

I can hear her open the door, her bright voice as she signs for a delivery. I turn her planner towards me and read through a scrawl of meetings and appointments. When her footsteps come down the hall, I return the planner to its position. "Sorry," she says. "Right. Do your parents have any favourite foods?"

"My mum loves crêpes." She made brown-butter crêpes for us on special occasions.

"And your father?"

101

"He likes the classics, steaks, chips, roasts." He also liked rabbit mousse terrine. There must be something wrong with a person who likes that.

Alice nods. She has a dent above her eyebrow, a small white scar, from chicken pox, maybe. You can't see it in her pictures, only at this distance. She tells me about some of her past events, asks about my budget, explains the terms of the contract, offers to send me a sample menu. Once we've gone through all the details, I thank her and push back my chair.

"What about you?" she asks as she walks me out. "What do you do?"

"I'm a GP." I stand on her front step and Alice leans in the doorway while asking about my practice. We talk for long enough that the dog comes outside and sits on her haunches next to us.

Alice seems kind. I noticed that at the event last week, and again tonight. If it's genuine, all of this might be unnecessary. I didn't need to make up an event, or lie to her. If I tell her who I am, she might help me.

Alice kneels to pull a burr from the dog's coat. I'll tell her the next time we see each other, I think, after I've figured out how to begin. "Right, I should get home," I say.

"Yes, sorry to keep you. I'll talk to you soon."

From the corner, I turn back to see Alice on her doorstep, her arm out, waving the dog inside.

On my way to the tube, I call Robbie's mobile. He texted me yesterday that he'd arrived in Lancashire but was too busy to talk.

He's a contract worker. Most of the time he's on his own, viewing the damaged homes, conducting interviews, filling in the stacks of paperwork for every claim. No one at the firm knows that he's taking six hundred milligrams of tramadol a day. It's not like alcohol, you can't see or smell it on him, unless you know what to look for. It must be exhausting for him, keeping it hidden.

He was off it for three days in hospital, maybe he hasn't started again. He's still young. This might be how it is for the rest of his life, or he might stop. Some people do stop.

I turn onto Fulham Road as the call goes to his voicemail. A few minutes later, I'm moving through a crowd outside Tesco when my phone rings. "Hi, Claire," says Robbie, and I smile, my head tilting towards his voice.

"Hey. How's Lancashire?"

"Good," he says. "Well, sort of, parts of it are under four feet of water." His tone is light, but I know. There's something just slightly artificial in his voice, like he's performing a very close imitation of the conversations we used to have. As soon as I hear it, my skin turns cold.

Robbie tells me about one of the houses he's already assessed, and its owners, and I stop to listen, the heel of my hand pressed against my forehead.

"I should go," he says. "I'm outside the next house."

"How does it look?" I ask, stalling.

"It's by a river," he says, "so not good."

I walk the rest of the way to the station, swipe my travel card, and go down the escalator to the platform. When the train arrives, my carriage is nearly empty. I find a seat and close my eyes.

At home, I research addiction treatments, old ones and new ones. I read about electro-acupuncture, methadone, eye desensitization, equine therapy, ayahuasca ceremonies.

The ayahuasca ceremonies are interesting. You fly to Peru

or Mexico, to a shamanic retreat, and drink a tea made from ayahuasca leaves, you purge for hours, vomiting and feverish, then begin to hallucinate. You return changed, according to the dozens of people whose accounts I've read, who arrived addicted to heroin, painkillers, alcohol, and have been sober since the ceremony.

The trouble is Robbie doesn't want to go. I wish I could do it for him. I'd do the unpleasant part, the purge, every hour for a year if it would help him. It's not fair, that he has this and I don't. I'm seven years older than my brother. Maybe that's why I'm doing better than he is now, like being loved by Mum was an incubator that was switched off too early for him.

———

I'M AT WORK when a message from Alice comes through with a menu, budget and contract. She's included a cake made of layers of crêpes, for Mum, presumably. I sign the contract and follow the directions for sending her a deposit. Telling the truth and asking for her help seemed so reasonable at her house on Thursday, but she's close to her parents, she will have grown up with their version of events. She has no reason to believe me instead of them.

The deposit has just gone through when a man appears in the doorway of my consulting room. "Gil, come in, how are you?"

He leans his walking stick against a chair. "I've caught a head cold, I think."

"Any fever?"

"No."

"Will you stand for me? I'll just have a listen to your lungs."

During my morning appointments, I examine a baby's rash and prescribe a steroid cream, I write a sick note for a man who has pulled a muscle in his back, I talk to a student about her panic attacks and give her the number for counselling. I check a man's prostate, which is swollen, and refer him to the hospital for screening, I look inside a toddler's reddened ear and write a prescription for an antibiotic.

Maeve is my last patient of the morning. She sits upright, with her hands in her lap and her lips pressed hard enough to turn them white. Her eyes haven't left my face since she came in, since she sat down. She's wearing a gold ring shaped like a hare, and I wonder if she put it on this morning for luck.

"It's good news, Maeve, it's benign." Her eyes water. I smile, handing her the tissues, and fiddle with her paperwork to give her a moment to absorb the news. "If you want to have the cyst removed because it bothers you, we can talk about that, but it isn't anything worrying."

After Maeve leaves, I carry my phone into the staff kitchen and check my messages while making coffee. Robbie hasn't called, but Alice has. It seems impossible to talk to her here, like some rule would prevent it, but then I've dialled and she's saying hello. "I got your contract," she says. "You're happy with the menu?"

"I did think of one thing. My dad likes the cream doughnuts at St John, could you do something similar?"

"Sure," she says, and I can hear a pen scratching, "though I haven't had those, I've still never been to St John."

I already knew that, of course, I read it in a comment under one of her pictures. "It's right by my flat, do you want to go sometime?"

"I'd love to," says Alice. "What about lunch this weekend?"

As we're saying goodbye, Laila and Anton come into the room. I slip my phone into the pocket of my cardigan and sit at the table with them, talking, until the idea of seeing Alice seems distant, nothing to make me nervous.

At half past noon on Saturday, I walk down St John Street. It ends at Smithfield Market, the old slaughterhouse, now a vast butchery. Alice is waiting outside the restaurant in sandals and a red cotton dress. The restaurant's sign, white tin streaked with rust, hangs above her. We kiss hello. "Is there a wait?"

"No, they have a table."

The dining room has whitewashed brick walls and black Cold War–era lamps. A skylight high above us is held closed with metal chains. Alice looks around with appreciation. "Are you drinking?" she asks.

I shrug. "I'm not on call."

"Let's get a bottle of wine, then," she says, and her voice is so relaxed that I wonder if part of her does remember me. She can't have much of a memory of me, but maybe I'm still familiar. While waiting for our food to arrive, we talk about my neighbourhood, and hers. "Have you been in Chelsea long?"

"Only a year. I used to live in California."

I tear a piece of bread, and remind myself that I'm not supposed to already know this. "Really? What part?"

"San Francisco." She tells me how much she misses Northern California, and being able to camp on the coast or in the mountains. I tell her about camping in Glen Coe in the Highlands, which Nell and I have done every summer since we were seventeen.

"Why did you come back?" I ask.

"To be near my parents. It was hard to be so far away." She lifts her wine glass. "And last spring my mum got sick."

"Oh, I'm so sorry. How is she now?"

"Good, we think. She had breast cancer, but her last two tests were clear."

My stomach drops. I imagine Rose during and after chemotherapy sessions, I imagine how scared Alice must have been, must still be. I think of Maeve and my other patients, waiting to hear their biopsy results, their backs straight, their knuckles whitening. I look at my lap, at the skylight, at Alice. "That must have been difficult."

"She's back at work now," says Alice. "That was the worst part for her, having to stay at home."

"What does she do?"

"She's a barrister."

I once sat on a bench across from her chambers in Inner Temple and watched Rose carry a box file to her desk. She was wearing a pressed white shirt and tortoiseshell reading glasses, and I stayed while she lifted papers from the box and began to annotate them.

"Did you always want to be a doctor?" asks Alice.

"No," I say, "it was more of a sudden decision." We talk about medical school and university. She asks me about friends of hers who were at the University of Edinburgh in my year.

"No, but I'm better with faces than names." I would have avoided her friends. I avoided the Eton students, the Harrow and

Bedales and Cheltenham students. Not that it was difficult, they only wanted to spend time with one another anyway.

She asks about siblings, and I tell her I have a younger brother who's working in Lancashire now, which feels like another lie, even though it's all I'd tell most people about him.

We order two cream doughnuts, and after tasting one, Alice nods. "We can make these."

"Oh, good."

She yawns. "Sorry. I was up early for a Pilates class."

I ask if she likes Pilates and she says, "No, it's awful, I miss exercising outdoors."

I remember the racquet leaning against her fence and say, "Me too, I used to play tennis, but all of my friends seem to have given it up."

"There's a court by my parents' house," she says. "Do you want to play sometime?"

"I would, actually."

We say goodbye outside the restaurant, the damp air carrying a ferrous smell up the road from Smithfield's. Alice has her back to the butcher's, and behind her, a man in rubber boots is hosing down the pavement.

On the walk back to my flat, I wonder if Alice has seen the documentary about my father that was broadcast two years ago. Rose appeared in it, in old news footage, leaving the coroner's court in a tweed skirt and silk blouse, her hair pinned up with a gold clip. Alice must have been curious, she must have wanted to know why her parents were involved.

It took me a long time to finish the documentary. I had to take a lot of breaks. The worst part was seeing the crime-scene picture of Emma. She was lying on her back with her head turned, and the floor around her was smeared with black stains. Some of the stains were small and regular. I'd made them, I realized. They were my footprints.

18

THERE WAS NEVER a trial for my father—he'd vanished, and you can't try a man in his absence—but there was a coroner's inquest, held to determine the circumstances of Emma's death. During my second year at university, I requested a transcript of the inquest from the public records office in London. It arrived in my postbox at the student centre on a cold, sleeting day in February. I took the envelope to my lectures, then carried it into an empty classroom to read.

The coroner's court was in Westminster, on Horseferry Road. In the quiet classroom, I wrote that down. I'd thought taking notes would make it easier, but already the inside of my cheek was raw from biting down on it. It was only dusk, though the heating seemed to have switched off for the night, and I sat reading the transcript in my coat.

The coroner interviewed the paramedics, officers, and forensic pathologists who'd seen Emma that night or examined our house afterwards. Since Emma didn't die of natural causes, he also interviewed detectives, neighbours, witnesses, friends of hers and our family, and Mum.

He conducted the interviews in a public court, acting as a sort of judge and prosecutor. I couldn't read the first part of the transcript, when he interviewed the pathologist about the post-mortem. The second part, the testimony from the paramedic, was also difficult. My jaw clamped, and I put my knuckle between my teeth, the way I did at night to stop grinding them.

I couldn't imagine Mum sitting in the coroner's court, listening to this testimony with my father's friends in the rows behind her. A few years before, I'd seen the famous picture of Mum that made it look like she'd come to the coroner's inquest in bare feet. She was on a bench outside the court, in a blue dress, without shoes. Her dress was a few inches too short and made of a bright, shiny material, like a satin nightdress, and she had a remote, dazed smile. She looked casual and eerily girlish, with her hands on either side of the bench and her legs swinging. Her feet were wrong too, the heels rough and cracked, and the nails done in orange varnish. The picture had been reprinted thousands of times.

She'd told me her shoes were too tight, she'd only slipped out of them for a moment. But her bare feet and glassy eyes made her look disturbed, unstable, unwell, all the words his friends had used for her.

Before the inquest, Rose, James, Sam and the rest of their friends had given press interviews saying Mum was sick. According to them, she'd hired someone to kill Emma and framed my father. They often mentioned that Mum's wounds were on the front of her body, and found a doctor to say that yes, in theory, all of her injuries could have been self-inflicted.

And they said dozens of other things to make the accusation more believable, like that she was greedy over his money. That she was so volatile she'd once smeared her menstrual blood on the wall after an argument. That she had strange sexual tastes, that she liked to wear PVC bodysuits and use an electric cattle prod during sex.

One of his friends said Mum talked with her mouth full. I'd never seen her do that, but it was a clever thing to say, it was small enough to sound true. They must have enjoyed it. Sitting in a room at the Clermont, inventing more and more lurid tastes for her. His friends had always loved parlour games.

I understood why they worked so hard to discredit her. If my father were convicted, the Frasers could be on trial for harbouring a fugitive or conspiracy to commit murder, and his other friends might be damaged by their association with him. The forensic results proved that my father was at the scene, but not that he had attacked the women—none of his skin under either of their finger-nails, no ripped hairs—so the main evidence against him would be Mum, she was the only witness. They wanted to make sure no one would believe a word she said.

During the break in the inquest, Mum ate alone in the canteen, while his friends went to the pub across the road. She might have been able to see them, laughing and talking at tables crowded with pints and orders of chips.

I didn't know why Mum went to the inquest alone, if no one had told her that she was allowed to bring a companion, or if she had thought watching someone else listening to it would be even worse.

After the break, the coroner interviewed Rose. In the transcript, I read Rose's description of my father's arrival at Ashdown on the night of the murder, and the account he gave her of walking past the house and seeing a fight inside. The coroner asked, "Why was Lord Spenser passing the house?"

Rose said, "He was worried about his children."

"Why?"

"He didn't think his wife was a fit mother."

"Why not?"

"Faye had a difficult time after her daughter's birth," said Rose. "She once told me she didn't trust herself near the baby with a knife."

My body jerked, like my foot had caught on the edge of a kerb. I didn't want to be in the classroom anymore, with its burners and bottles of hydrogen peroxide, the smell of it coating the back of my throat. I hurried out of the building onto Buccleuch Street and started to walk towards the Grassmarket. Edinburgh was dark, and busy with people on their way home from work or school. I wanted to stop someone and ask for help. It didn't make sense that I couldn't call Mum and ask, Did you want to hurt me? Did you wish you'd never had me?

I didn't know then what I do now about post-natal disorders. A lot of mothers have thoughts of dropping their baby on the stairs, drowning them in the bath, pushing their pram into the road. It doesn't mean they'll do it, or that they secretly want to. The thoughts are a way of testing themselves, making sure their child is safe.

But I doubt Mum knew that at the time. I imagine the thoughts tortured her, that she worried there was something wrong with her, that she shouldn't be left alone with me. She must have gone to Rose for help, and this is what Rose did with what she'd told her.

19

I PRACTISE HITTING against the wall by the public courts near my house. It's been years since I played tennis, and I wonder how good she'll be. Alice learned on the court at Ashdown. It's something we have in common, my father taught me to play there. He was a good teacher, he didn't become impatient even when I hit the ball over the hedge and we had to go and search for it.

It's starting to get dark, and the strip lights have come on in the stairwell of the council block above the court. My next swing misses, and Jasper chases after the ball.

I wonder if my father still plays tennis. I often wonder how he's kept busy. He used to be a member of the Beaufort hunt, maybe he's bought a horse. He must have missed it. They rode all day sometimes, twenty horses and riders in black coats, galloping across a field. Or he's learned how to cook. Or taken up painting. These thoughts always make me furious, and I keep hitting until my arms and back burn.

*

Alice is already on the other side of the fence when I arrive. Burton Court is private, she has to come and unlock the gate for me. I shade my eyes to look across the vast green lawn surrounding the tennis courts. This amount of space, in the centre of Chelsea, seems even more improbable from inside the fence. "What was this originally?"

"A parade ground, I think. The Royal Hospital owns it now." Alice is wearing white shorts and a maroon jumper with varsity stripes. The jumper looks old, it might be hers from school. Ahead of us, two women are playing in white pleated skirts. I'm wearing leggings and a grey top, I hadn't realized people actually wore tennis whites.

"Which one's your parents' house?" I ask, and she points across the field to a townhouse covered in ivy. We're too far to see into the rooms, I can just make out the gold knocker on the front door.

"Want to volley first?" she asks. The ball floats back and forth over the net. When it rolls away, I look to the townhouse. It's Saturday morning, her parents might be at home.

Alice is the better player, but she's rustier. Presumably she didn't spend this week practising, though she still wins two of the three sets. Afterwards, we're breathless, and the fine hairs around her face have curled in the heat. She says, "We'll sleep well tonight."

That sensation, like a defibrillator shock. It was one of Mum's stock phrases. She always said it after we'd spent the day on the beach, or hiking on the coast path, and hearing it made me inordinately proud.

I need my mum. I need her to tell me what to do about Robbie. He's still in Lancashire, he won't be back in London for at least another month, and I hate thinking of him alone in a hotel. At least he's busy, the firm makes its assessors work long hours after a storm.

As we cross the lawn to the gate, Alice tells me a story about her father. I listen, and ask questions. I think, I spent three months watching your father. I followed him to his office, his house, a train station. I watched him enter a spa for a massage and waited until he came out.

After we say goodbye, Alice walks to the King's Road for a cab, and I go the other way, past her parents' house. The wind has lifted and the ivy courses on its front wall. I look at the fanlight and remember watching James roll a suitcase to the door the last time I was here.

James has known my father since boarding school. They went to Eton together, along with Sam. I visited Eton once, as part of my research. My father was happy there. What does it do to you, to go to a school where you live in a house with a tradesman's entrance? Where you have a three-course dinner prepared for you every night, ending with biscuits and a cheeseboard? Where tourists come to photograph you? It must have an effect. You must expect things to go a certain way for you. He couldn't have planned a murder, I don't think, without that confidence. He thought he would get away with it.

At Eton, he and James lived in Godolphin, and Sam was nearby in Waynflete. They were together for six years, from age thirteen to eighteen. When my father needed their help two decades later, .they must have been pleased at the chance to prove themselves. They couldn't, as children, have invented a better scenario for testing their courage and loyalty. If they had been caught helping my father leave the country, they would have gone to prison. They chose to help him and not to protect themselves. I imagine they still like to think about this, to go over every detail in their minds, and that the memory warms them.

I continue past the Frasers' house and turn down Flood Street. I call Robbie again, but he doesn't answer, and I try as hard as I can not to picture his phone ringing in his pocket while he lies unconscious.

20

W HEN I WAS SIXTEEN, Mum brought a computer home from her office. Her boss had said he was going to throw it away since they'd ordered new ones. It needed to be restarted often, and the dial-up was so slow that I usually had time to go downstairs and make a snack while a page loaded. Robbie had taken to humming the sound of the modem dialling as he went past my room.

I'd known, as soon as Mum carried it through the door, what the computer meant, and had considered telling her I didn't want it, or shoving it off the desk to the floor.

I'd never searched for information about my father before. I could have asked the librarian in Crail for help finding articles about him, or used the computer lab at school, but not with any privacy. And I wanted to know less about that night, not more. For a year afterwards, I had trouble walking without jerking and catching myself, like something was under my feet.

A week after she brought home the computer, Mum said, "I have to pick up my new glasses in St Andrews, want to come?"

While she waited at the optometrist's, I walked to my favourite university building, the gothic stone hall at the edge of town, above the sea, which held Moral Philosophy and Logic and Metaphysics. My exam results were good, so far. I might be applying to St Andrews the next year. I might take a class in this building, on logic and metaphysics. The thought made me happy, even though I had almost no idea what such a class would cover.

A group of girls with soft leather backpacks and high, clear accents came down the road, and I turned away. My old school, Francis Holland, sent a lot of girls to St Andrews, and I was scared of running across one of them.

Even if they had been from Francis Holland, they probably wouldn't have recognized me. It had been eight years. After the inquest, we moved to Crail, a fishing village on the coast north of Edinburgh. No one there had recognized us. Before we moved, Mum dyed her hair auburn and changed its cut. She'd gained weight too, she wasn't frail anymore. And she dressed differently. That day she was wearing jeans and a soft, faded leopard-print coat.

I walked back through campus to the high street. At the bookshop, I used my babysitting money to buy a new hardback novel, which I showed to Mum and Robbie on our way to the Chinese restaurant. Mum ordered wonton soup, I had chow fun and most of Robbie's fried rice.

I didn't start my homework until after nine o'clock, and decided to do an hour, then go to bed and wake early to finish it. I began to outline a chapter from my physics textbook, then stood to close the door. I left the textbook open on my desk and turned on the computer.

I still wanted to forget everything about that night, and I was also typing his name. An image came into my mind of Emma's wet hair, and I stared at my textbook until it went away. Then I waited, for ages, as the first result loaded.

The site had small red font on a black screen and was divided into four sections: Background, Crime, Investigation and Aftermath.

I looked around my bedroom. The books on the bedside table, the heap of clothes on the floor, the posters, the cards stuck in the mirror. The hair rose on my arms, like whoever made the site was watching me, and would be adding all of this under Aftermath.

My tongue felt swollen and stripped, like I'd eaten too many sweets. I'd known there would be things online about my family, but not how many. The site had a forum with dozens of active members. Its creator, someone named Neil, began the section on the crime with a description of what we'd eaten for dinner that night.

I stopped reading, and went across the hall to Mum's room. Her slippers were next to the bed, and her body rose and fell under the blanket. I thought about waking her up, but didn't know what I would say.

Downstairs was dark except for the lights on the Christmas tree. They were set to a timer, which never worked. I moved to the window. Someone had already come to put salt on the road, since it was supposed to snow in the night.

I checked the lock on the front door. All of the people on the forum liked researching us. I wondered if any of them had figured out where we lived.

Through the window, Crail looked the same as usual. The small houses across the road had wreaths on their doors and strands of coloured Christmas lights. Those houses backed onto the sea, and they hung lights there too for the fishermen.

I lifted our dog, Finn, from the sofa and carried him upstairs with me. He curled in a circle on my bed, and I sat at my desk and thought, You can stop when it gets to the bad part.

My father ate dinner before he came to our house, I learned. The police found dishes in his sink.

Earlier that day he'd gone to work, according to the site. He sat in meetings, returned calls, and ran out in the afternoon to collect a suit from a tailor on Conduit Street. At six, he returned to his flat. He talked on the phone to his cousin and bought a paper from the newsagent's. One of his neighbours saw him; he'd changed out of his work clothes into a pearl-grey cotton polo shirt.

Then he made dinner. He wasn't too nervous to eat. I couldn't imagine what was in his mind. How did he know he'd be able to do it?

I wanted to know what he was thinking when he walked to our house and climbed the back wall. If he was scared. If he almost turned back. If the garden looked strange to him, or familiar. He'd spent so much time in it. He'd planted all of the trees and shrubs that he walked past on the way to the door.

How long did he stand outside? From the garden, he would have been able to see a woman sitting at the kitchen counter, with her back to him, under a pendant lamp. He must have thought she was Mum.

He broke the lock. That part must have happened quickly, since Emma didn't have time to run. She reached across the counter for a knife and knocked the draining rack to the floor. Reading about him hitting her made my teeth chatter and my mouth fill with water. It was an effort to swallow, and to breathe.

Emma managed to turn around. Her face would have had blood on it by then, but not enough to hide her features. He must have seen that she was the wrong woman. He could have stopped, but instead he lifted the pipe again.

He knew I was upstairs. Did he think I wouldn't hear? Or had he known I'd be too much of a coward to come down?

The police found the dinner dishes in his sink and a rag dropped on the counter. He hadn't cleaned his flat or packed a bag, he must have expected to return home afterwards, that he was going to shower, throw away his stained clothing, practise his alibi, get away with it.

He must have done so much research. He wasn't an idiot, he'd have known the police would suspect him, and that he'd need to create some other, plausible explanation. If it had worked, I realized, he would have custody of me and Robbie. We would have gone to live with him, and never known what he had done.

"You were up late last night," said Mum. She was at the kitchen table in jeans and a red-and-black-checked flannel shirt.

"What?"

"I heard you go to the bathroom."

"I had a lot of homework."

She nodded and reached around me for the coffee. Did she know what I'd been reading? She was good at that sort of thing. She often set out aspirin before I mentioned having a headache.

Mum yawned, put bread in the toaster, went to the back door and said, "Wasn't it supposed to snow last night?"

No, I thought, she doesn't know. Robbie came in and Mum offered him a piece of toast. He said, "I'm not hungry."

"Have some and I'll finish the rest," said Mum. He was small for his age, she was always trying to get him to eat more pasta, butter, cream.

I ate my breakfast. Across the table, Robbie attempted to return his piece of toast to Mum. A brass cookie cutter in the shape of a heart hung on the wall behind him, and a row of Russian nesting dolls was lined up on the windowsill. Everything in the room was so familiar, but so was the house in Belgravia.

Finn was begging at the table. He was a Skye terrier, like Greyfriars Bobby, the dog who waited by his master's grave for fourteen years. Whenever we went into Edinburgh, I tried to convince Nell to visit the dog's statue with me, which she only agreed to because the pub next to it, also called Greyfriars Bobby, served us sometimes.

I fed Finn and gathered my schoolbooks. While I put on my shoes, Mum was talking on the phone with Sabrina in Wales, as she did every morning. She said, "Claire, your shirt's inside out." Into the phone, she said, "Whose goats?"

Before Robbie and I left, I waved to Mum, who waved back, distracted, covering the mouthpiece of the phone with her hand even though she wasn't saying anything.

*

Nell spent the bus ride hunched over a worksheet. "Why didn't you do that last night?" I asked, and she sighed. The paper was grey at the edges and torn. Nell has four siblings, and most of her belongings came out of the house tattered.

She chewed the side of her thumb. "What about this one?"

"Factor that part out."

"How does it factor?"

"X plus y, x minus y."

She finished the last question and tightened her ponytail. A tractor went by us, pouring glittering salt onto the road before the snowstorm. Nell said, "Do you think we'll be let out early?"

I looked at the other students on the bus and wondered what would happen if they found out who I was. The girls at Francis Holland had stopped talking to me. Every single one. When Mum picked me up from school, I made sure to time my exit so it looked like I was leaving with a group of other girls. Sometimes I turned around, or waved, so I seemed to be saying goodbye to a friend.

The reaction would be different here. Some of them might like me more because of it, which would be even worse.

21

A LICE AND I have developed a routine. We play tennis on Saturday morning and then walk to Orange Square, where we both have an iced coffee and a Danish at a table outside the café.

We have enough in common never to run out of things to talk about, especially since I've studied her photos. I try not to seem overly familiar, though, to maintain a level of reserve. We talk mostly about work, restaurants, books, travel. I've researched certain destinations so I can discuss them with her. Positano, Courchevel, the Maldives. I tell myself that this isn't entirely lying, since my parents brought me to some of these places when I was little, I just don't remember them.

I don't go abroad often. My father has ruined foreign travel for me. I spend the entire time wondering if he lives there. In a train or car, I stare out of the window at foreign villages, foreign houses, demented with not knowing if he's inside.

Recently Alice and I have started to talk about relationships, which is a relief, since I don't have to invent any of it. She asked if I ever want to get married, and I said no. I didn't say, Would you, if you had my parents?

"What about you?" I asked. "Why did your last relationship end?"

"I had a call from his girlfriend."

"No," I said, and Alice nodded. "I thought you said you were living together."

"We were. His company has an office in Seattle, he spent half his time there. We figured out that he'd been talking about marriage with both of us. I think he would have just kept it going. I might have found out when we were seventy that he had another family."

"Christ."

"Not the best year," said Alice, tearing her Danish in half.

I think that she likes me, but also that I fill a role for her. She hasn't been back in London very long. Her best friend lives in California, and most of her friends here have just had children, she doesn't seem to see much of them.

After tennis, we usually only stay in Ebury Square for as long as it takes to finish our coffees. Though one time I walked across the square with her to buy some flowers, and another time we shared a newspaper.

This morning I told her I had to pick up some groceries at the overpriced shop on the square, and she said, "I'll come with you, I should get it over with now too."

She ordered four steaks at the butcher's counter. "It's my dad's birthday tonight," she said. "I'm cooking dinner at their house." She's an only child, I wonder who the fourth guest will be.

*

While Alice cooks dinner for her father's birthday, I meet Nell at a Chinese restaurant on Wardour Street. She came to London this morning for work, and has a few hours before catching the sleeper train to Edinburgh.

It starts to rain, and the window by our table fogs over. I wonder if Alice will still use the outdoor grill. I picture her under an umbrella, using a pair of tongs to turn the steaks, while her parents and their guest have a drink inside. Nell is looking at me. "What?" I say.

"I asked if you need to borrow a sleeping bag."

I don't know what she's talking about. We stare at each other over the table, then I remember, with a turn in my stomach, that we're supposed to go camping in Glen Coe in July.

"Nell, I'm so sorry. I can't go this year."

"Very funny."

"No, really." I don't want to lie to her, but if I explain about Alice, she'll be even angrier. "I can't leave work."

"Didn't you already ask for the days off?"

"Harriet's about to go on maternity leave," I say, which is true. "Everyone has to cover for her."

"Can we go in September, then?"

I nod, though I can't imagine that far away yet, I don't know when things with Alice will come to a head. I apologize again, a waiter comes with our wine, and Nell takes a long drink of it. I ask about her meetings. Nell translates Swedish books for a few London publishing houses. She shows me a new manuscript, with notes from her meeting in the margins.

Our dim sum arrives, and we eat greedily, fighting over the dish of plum sauce. Nell pours us more wine. I'm in an old jumper and haven't put on any makeup, and I doubt Nell has noticed what I'm wearing. I'm so glad to be with her. It's like an alarm sounding in a room has suddenly been switched off. I didn't realize how distressing it would be, pretending to be someone else. Every time I see Alice, I'm lying to her. I thought it would be like following James, but I like Alice, she isn't the same as her parents.

"Did you finish painting the house?" I ask, and Nell nods. I visit her often, and know her home as well as mine. The one floorboard under the straw mat that creaks, the ferns on the bathroom windowsill to look at while you have a shower, the red enamel fridge.

Nell tells me about a new bar in Merchiston, and it makes me homesick, desperate to walk down Morningside Road, with the black Pentland Hills in the distance.

"How's Robbie?" she asks.

"The same."

"Has he had any more seizures?"

"No, but he's at more of a risk now that he's had one."

"Where is he buying it? Does he still have a prescription?"

"No, online."

"Have you thought about telling the police?"

"He'd never forgive me."

"I think he'd understand eventually," Nell says. "Given the other option."

After we finish our dinner, I take a cab with her to King's Cross. On the concourse, she says, "My friend's practice is looking for a new GP."

"Where?"

"Edinburgh, somewhere in New Town. Want to send her your CV?"

"I'll think about it."

Nell waves from the end of the platform, then she climbs onto the train and I walk down to the tube.

———————

I'M FINISHING PAPERWORK at the practice when my mobile rings. There's a long spell of static, and then Robbie says, "Hi, Claire."

My chest tightens. I haven't heard his voice in weeks, he's only texted me. "Hi, Robbie."

The static comes again, and a humming. He says, "Can I stay at your place tonight?"

"Of course, where are you?"

"On the train. We're by Coventry."

"Okay, see you soon."

I have an hour of forms left, but will finish them in the morning. It's drizzling outside, and I fumble with my umbrella. Coventry is at least an hour away, but I still walk so fast I'm nearly running. I have to get home, I have to get everything ready. Robbie might be hungry. I stop at the health store near my house and order a takeaway, a rice bowl with tempeh and vegetables. He likes soy sauce; I ask for extra packets.

I walk to Marks and Spencer and fill a trolley with groceries, with fresh food, but also frozen pizzas and crisps. He needs the fat, he weighs less now than he did when he was fourteen. What would Mum say if she knew that?

I know some of what he eats. Loaves of soft white bread, packets of powdered doughnuts, marked-down tins of soup. He doesn't have much of an appetite from the tramadol. He must be hungry a lot of the time, but not notice.

At home, I set the takeaway on the counter. It takes me a while to put away all the groceries, I never buy this much in one trip. I switch on the lamps, and find a clean set of towels, and sheets for making up the sofa. And then I wait. I try to read, and listen for the buzzer. Some cabs drive by in the wet, but none stop. I keep checking my mobile. The takeaway has gone cold, and I'm putting it in the fridge when the buzzer sounds.

Robbie is standing on the doorstep. I hug him, and with my chin hooked on his shoulder say, "It's good to see you. Why did the trip take so long?"

"Broken rail," he says. I take him in at a glance. He's shaky on his feet, and all of his movements seem to require special attention.

Upstairs, he stands near the door with his backpack on. His hair is wet and plastered to his head, and his shoes are soaked through. He looks around my flat, and I wonder if he hates me for it. When he crouches down to pet Jasper, the dog is ecstatic, he always remembers him.

Robbie rents a room in a flatshare in Peckham. Someone might be staying in it, he might have sublet it while he was away for work, or he just doesn't want to go back there yet. I won't ask, I don't want him to feel unwelcome. Robbie tugs at his jacket pocket, like he's having trouble getting something out of it. After a while, he extracts a folded gum wrapper, considers it, returns it to his pocket.

"Do you want to have a shower?" I ask, and he nods. "I can wash your clothes."

"I'll do it." Robbie removes them from his backpack and holds them against his chest. I listen to him close the machine and pour in detergent. He shuffles into the bathroom, and stays in the shower for a long time. "I used your face mask," he says afterwards.

I laugh. "Did you?"

"Can't you tell?"

"Are you hungry?"

He says, "I could eat." He forms each word carefully, like his mouth is full of marbles.

I heat up the takeaway. He sits on the sofa with the plate on his knees. The food seems to be gone in a few bites, I should have got two.

We make up the pullout bed on the sofa. I bought the sofa with him in mind. He was still living in Bristol then, and I wanted a spare bed for when he visited. He sits up against the pillows, and Jasper lies across his legs. "Are you still hungry? I have more, I did a shop recently."

Robbie shakes his head. I make us mugs of hot chocolate anyway, with double cream instead of milk. He's so thin. He smiles a little to himself when I hand him the hot chocolate, and I think, I'm pushing too much.

"Do you have to go back to Lancashire?"

"No, we're done."

We watch a sitcom. Next to me on the sofa Robbie laughs soundlessly, with his shoulders shaking and his hand curled a few inches in front of his face. He seems different, less frenetic, and his voice sounds different too, it's not strangled or flattened.

He says, "I don't think I should be in London at the moment."

I stay very still. "Where do you want to go?"

"Penbridge."

"All right. We'll call in the morning."

We say good night. I close my door and climb into bed. He wants to go to a rehab, he's asking me to take him. This hasn't happened before. He's only ever tried to stop on his own.

I wake early. I have to call Penbridge. If they don't have a bed, there are plenty of others. I have a spreadsheet of them saved on my computer.

Sunshine fills my bedroom. I can't hear if Robbie's awake yet. I open the door and moan. His sheets are folded on the sofa. His plate and cup are rinsed and set on the draining rack.

22

IN CRAIL, I babysat for a family called the Fennells almost every week. They lived on Marketgate in a large stone house with a stepped roof. One evening, I waited on their step with my hands in my coat pockets, looking at the wreath on their front door.

"Hi, Claire," said Rebecca. "Thanks for coming. Freezing out, isn't it?" She asked about my classes while putting on a pair of heels, her voice warm and familiar. We knew each other well, I'd started babysitting for them two years before, when I turned fourteen.

Max and Lucy ran into the hall and attached themselves to my legs. After their parents left, we played a board game. Max went to sleep on his own, and I read to Lucy in bed from *The Borrowers* while she leaned against me. I wondered if her parents would still let me babysit if they knew about my father.

Once Lucy fell asleep, I went downstairs and opened the fridge. There was gourmet pizza, and containers of risotto and gnocchi and fish pie from an expensive deli in Edinburgh. I didn't want to leave an obvious absence in the fridge, so instead I ate small amounts from a lot of different things, which, I realized, would seem even stranger to them if they noticed.

I did my homework, then wandered through their house, which was larger than ours, and had polished hardwood floors and Berber rugs. In the master bathroom, I looked at Rebecca's jars, simple white tubs with French names. They were different from Mum's products, the clay masks and peppermint foot rubs that she bought on offer at the Co-op.

My eyes had pouches under them. I hadn't slept well for the past week, since visiting the website about my father. I used some of Rebecca's eye cream, which only seemed to make the pouches shiny as well as swollen.

A pile of black, navy, and cream cashmere jumpers was folded on Rebecca's bed. I shouldn't like them, I thought. I didn't want to have anything in common with my father. Which also meant I couldn't like horses, or yachts, or villas, though none of those seemed to be in the offing.

My friends at school were so careless with their infractions. They could be greedy, they could gossip and lie without thinking. I couldn't. My father was a liar, I wouldn't be anything like him.

I left the bedroom and went down to watch television. The Fennells paid for all the expensive channels, and I watched *The Thirty-Nine Steps*. I always chose differently in their house, like they would somehow know what I'd seen and judge me based on it. Or maybe these were my real preferences, and their nice house suited me better. I hoped not, that it was just that usual mixture, how you're both more relaxed and more guarded in someone else's house.

When I came home, Mum was in the sitting room. I dropped onto the sofa next to her, and she said, "How was it?"

"Good. They went to bed at eight and I watched *The Thirty-Nine Steps*."

"I haven't seen that in years. Did you like it?"

I nodded, shifting against her. "Rebecca Fennell has really nice jumpers."

Mum laughed. "I bet she does."

I wanted to tell her the rest. They were cashmere, I wanted to try them on, does that mean I'm greedy, does that mean I'm like him, do I remind you of him?

Mum patted my arm. She said, "I'm going to bed. Will you remember to turn off the Christmas lights?"

"Yes."

"You forgot last night."

"I won't."

I tried to read more about my father online, but couldn't concentrate. I kept thinking someone was in the house. I'd already gone downstairs twice to check the lock on the front door.

I was at the window, looking out at the row of streetlamps in the fog, when the idea came to me. I created an account on the forum, opened a new thread, and wrote, "Does anyone know where Faye and the children live now?"

I waited for replies for another hour, then tried to sleep.

*

The next morning, I ate breakfast at the kitchen table with Robbie, who was drawing up very precise plans for a gingerbread house, and Mum, who was reading the newspaper. I looked at her face and neck and arms. She didn't seem to have any scars from where he'd hit her. I'd read that during the attack he reached his hand down her throat. I wanted to ask if that had healed too, or if it still hurt sometimes.

"Can you take Finn out?" she asked. I walked him down the high street, past the striped awning of the East Neuk Hotel, where Nell and I worked as chambermaids in the summer, and around to the harbour. On the quay, some tourists were taking pictures of the lobstermen, which the lobstermen pretended not to notice.

I sat on one of the benches. White spray broke over the harbour walls, and I looked across the grey, heaving sea towards Denmark. There was a gale coming towards us. No one was supposed to drive tonight, and all the shops were closing early.

A couple walked past me and into Reilly Shellfish, and came out a few minutes later with plastic bags of ice and mussels. At sea, the rigging on the fog buoy clinked. I loved the sound, especially at night, when you couldn't see the buoy itself.

I pulled my boots onto the bench and wrapped my arms around my legs. Waves knocked against the hulls of the fishing boats, and a few pieces of driftwood floated on the water. We'd collect it from the beach after the gale. Mum liked to burn driftwood on the fire, she said it smelled better.

I don't want to leave, I thought, but if someone on the forum knows that we live here, I'll have to tell Mum, and we might have to move.

*

AT HOME, I opened the thread. "They moved to Ireland," said the first reply. "They live in Dalkey now."

I slumped back in my chair. Not our town, not even close. Someone else wrote, "Are you sure? Isn't Dalkey quite expensive?"

The people on the forum knew more about our finances than I did. My father hadn't taken any money from his accounts when he disappeared, apparently. The accounts were still shared with Mum then, since they hadn't started divorce negotiations yet, but she refused to take anything that was his. She signed the house and all of their shared assets over to my grandmother. Which explained why we'd had so little money in our first two years in Scotland, before Mum found her job at the chiropodist's office, and why she was still paying off credit card debt.

I kept checking the thread throughout the day, as more and more people posted answers. A few confirmed that we were in Ireland. One said, "My friend works with the police. They're definitely in Ireland, but in Wexford, not Dalkey."

No one mentioned Crail. I was so happy we could stay that I almost told Mum everything. The gale broke onshore, and I read a novel in my bedroom while listening to the salt rain lashing the roof. We were safe. No one was watching us, no one was checking the doors and windows when we were out.

23

ALICE IS WEARING a white cotton tennis dress, and the sun is strong enough to make a fuzz of glare around the fabric. I'm not playing well, I've been distracted all morning and keep making mistakes. We're both sweating, wiping our hands and foreheads before each serve. She wins the first set, and says, "Want to stop there?" I nod, using my teeth to open the water bottle.

Alice winces, and I ask, "Are you all right?"

"Just a headache. Do you have any aspirin?"

"Not with me."

"Do you mind if we stop at my parents' place?"

We walk across Burton Court to St Leonard's Terrace and her parents' house. I try to stay steady as Alice opens the gate, as we walk down the path to the front door and inside. I look at the carpeted staircase, the red dining room, the pile of envelopes on a sideboard. Alice leads me down the hall and into the kitchen, where a glass conservatory extends into the garden.

She checks a drawer, then sighs. "I'll be right back. There's lemonade in the fridge if you're still thirsty."

As she climbs the stairs, I open a cabinet and take down a glass. So this is what their house is like inside. Her parents read those newspapers crumpled on the table. They chose this set of china. That laptop belongs to one of them. I have trouble opening the bottle of lemonade, since my hands are slick with sweat.

The house's thick Georgian walls absorb sound, I can't tell where Alice is above me. I open the laptop. It asks for a password, and I'm trying to think of one they might use when a key scrapes in the lock. I move away from the laptop, towards the sink, as a tall, wiry man in a navy polo shirt comes into the room. He frowns when he sees me.

"Hi, I'm Claire. Alice is upstairs."

James considers me, and I'm aware that I'm sweating, that there are stains under my arms, that some of my hair is stuck to my forehead, that I'm a stranger in his house. He looks at the glass in my hand, and I want to say that Alice offered the lemonade, I didn't just help myself.

"She has a headache," I say, finally.

"She often does. Good match?"

"Not our best."

James stands with a slight stoop. His hair is thinning, I can see the reddish freckles across his scalp. He starts to sort through the post on the counter. I don't know what to do with my glass, if I should leave it in the sink or put it in the dishwasher. Either one seems presumptuous.

Alice comes back at last, says hello to her dad, takes a peach from a bowl, offers me one. "Ready?"

I set my glass in the sink and follow her outside, where Rose is in the front garden unpacking bags from a nursery. "This is my friend Claire," says Alice, and Rose gives me a distracted smile. I look at her and think, We were almost taken into care because of you.

Alice explains about the headache, the aspirin, and Rose says, "Are you still coming over this afternoon?"

Alice nods. "I might spend the night. I think I'm coming down with something."

"I'll ask your father to get Stella from your house. He has to drive over to Putney anyway," says Rose, and I have to stop myself from asking why.

Alice waves goodbye to her mum, and in a few minutes we're ordering at the café, and I feel sick thinking of how poorly that went.

At home, I take a beer from the fridge, then stand looking into it. I'd forgotten about all of this food, the frozen pizzas and soups, the fresh gnocchi and spring greens, the fruit, which I thought Robbie might like to press for juice. I'll never be able to eat it all on my own before it goes off.

A car alarm sounds in the road. I can hear voices from the flat below mine, and the night air is thick with ozone. I check the schedule for my on-call day, I start a load of laundry and make sure that I have clean suits for the week.

I've messed this up. The way James met me—alone inside his house, having made myself at home—could hardly have been worse. Both of her parents noticed my discomfort, I think. They might mention it to Alice. I can picture Rose saying, "Why do you need a new friend? You already have a cast of thousands."

James seems to have aged a lot recently. I find the picture, cut from a newspaper, of the Ramsden Club, eight young men in tailcoats, including my father, James and Sam. All of them look pleased with themselves. They'd made it through the initiation, after being chosen from all the undergraduate men at Oxford, they'd joined a club where members had become judges, actors, spies, foreign secretary, prime minister.

I read about one of their parties once. Its location was a secret, in a field somewhere outside Oxford. They brought guests, mostly girls, in on buses. All the guests were given white masks and dark robes. There were pigs' heads on stakes and a huge fire in the centre of their circle.

But it was just slightly too cold. And the masks fastened behind the head with elastic, which people found irritating. A few of the guests pushed the masks up onto their hair, like sunglasses. Some of the girls put coats on over their robes for warmth.

No one knew what to do. It seemed wrong in that setting to talk about exams, or gossip, or tell jokes, as one usually did at a party, but there wasn't a replacement activity on offer. Instead there was a lot of drifting around, standing by the fire, looking at the soapy skin on the pigs' heads.

Two of the Ramsden members wrestled in the mud by the fire, which was stirring at first, the flames jumping on their cold skin, their dark hair falling over their eyes, and then went on too long and became boring.

One of the bus drivers was sleeping in his seat, the other was reading a newspaper and working through a bag of crisps. Their complete indifference to the party was galling to the club members. They'd thought the bus drivers would want to watch, maybe even become too excited and have to be told off.

The guests grew hungry. No one had brought any food, they hadn't thought they'd need it. The party was meant to last until dawn, but by midnight most of the guests had begun to hitchhike back to Oxford.

Early the next morning, a boy from the party arrived at a hospital in Oxford with three broken ribs, but he refused to say what had happened to him. He's in Parliament now. I wonder where he would be if he'd told the truth.

24

G OOD NEWS," said Nell on the bus home from school. "Caitlin's brother's going to the Vix tonight."

"Does he have room in his car?"

"Sure," she said. At Caitlin's house, we ate cherry Haribo and drank vodka while getting ready. One of our friends had told me that if you filter cheap vodka five times, it tastes the same as the expensive brands. I remembered that every time I drank vodka, even though it wasn't particularly interesting, and I never planned on trying it.

"Close your eyes," Caitlin said, and dragged liner above my lashes. Nell changed the music, and traded me the vodka for the Haribo. Fat bubbles slid through the vodka when I lifted the bottle to my mouth.

Nell was wearing a grey vest top over a neon yellow bra, and I'd borrowed a short dress with a zip up the front. We put on our duffel coats, and I noticed that specific sensation, which you only ever have while going out in the winter, of bare arms against slippery coat lining.

Caitlin's brother and his friends were in the kitchen, also drinking Glen's, not eating Haribo. He looked at us. "I don't have room for three of you."

"We'll fit," said Nell.

"Hi," I said in the car to the boy whose lap I was sitting on.

"Hi," he said. "Are you comfortable?"

I nodded, took the vodka from Nell, drank, handed the bottle to him, hunching forward so he had enough room to manoeuvre it. Nell said, "Can you turn the music up?"

The boy whose lap I was sitting on said, "My name's Tom."

"I'm not driving you back if you don't get in," said Caitlin's brother.

"We'll be fine," said Caitlin. The three of us had gone to a head shop in Edinburgh to buy fake licences, which we'd tested at all the bars on the Grassmarket. The only place that hadn't let us in was a strip club. Which may have been a good thing, actually. Instead we went to the kebab shop next door and got into an argument about sex work. Nell said that it should be legalized, and sex workers celebrated. I said yes, but only if people entered into it by choice, not because they had no other options. She said, "What about people working in call centres? Should that be illegal unless they have other options?" "Definitely," I said, then Caitlin said, "If I get more chips will you have some?" and we both said yes.

Caitlin's brother parked the car, and we joined the queue outside the Vix. "Do you think we'll get in?" I asked Nell, and she nodded. "But we haven't used them here," I said.

"Stop it," she said.

We reached the door, and then the bouncer was returning my licence and I was following the others into the club. Nell ordered a vodka tonic, and I asked for the same. I used Nell as my pacer, like the cyclist in a marathon ahead of the runners. It seemed good for me to have one. I didn't think that my childhood had been the best preparation for setting limits.

At the bar, I talked to Tom about his history course. I breathed in, feeling my dress tighten around my ribs, the metal zip cool against my stomach and chest. Nell ordered two kamikaze shots for herself, and it occurred to me that I should have chosen someone else as my pacer. Using Nell was like having no pacer at all.

Tom and I went outside for a cigarette, then into the back seat of Caitlin's brother's car. When we came back in, Nell said, "Should I tell him he needs to get his car washed?" Tom and I nodded our heads, laughing. On the ride home, I drowsed on Nell's lap, with her arms linked around me.

I knew what the people on the forum would say if they'd seen me in the car with Tom. They would think I was putting myself in harm's way, like shagging a boy in the back seat of a car was dangerous. They would make it sound like I wanted something bad to happen to me, but the bad things had already happened, I wanted something good.

———

WHEN I CAME HOME from school on Monday, the house was empty. I kept my coat on while checking the rooms. No one had replied saying we were in Crail, but that didn't mean we were safe. My father had tried to kill my mum, and she was still alive. He might try again. Or one of his friends might. Or someone from the forum, like the man who'd posted a picture of a woman—not Mum, but she looked like her—naked with a metal ball stuffed in her mouth.

My bedroom door was open just wide enough for a person to be standing behind it. I pushed the door, holding my breath, waiting for it to swing back towards me. The handle knocked against the wall and I exhaled, then looked under the beds, inside the wardrobes, behind the shower curtain.

When Mum came home, I was studying at the kitchen table. She said, "What's the hammer doing there?"

The hammer was on the table, next to my textbooks and notes. I pointed at the floor. "Loose nail."

A hammer was apparently more reliable than a knife. You didn't have to worry as much about accuracy.

I wondered how hard it would be to get a hunting rifle. Most of the estates in the Highlands, a few hours north of us, had guns. People like my father's friends used them for shooting parties, and it wasn't fair that they had access to rifles and I didn't.

Years earlier I'd stayed in one of those houses in the Highlands. Sam's family had an estate near Inverness, and we'd visited for the Glorious Twelfth, the start of the shooting season.

They had a six-hundred-acre grouse moor. None of the children were allowed on the shooting party, but I remembered seeing them crossing the flank of a hill, small figures in flat caps and jackets, with guns like sticks over their shoulders.

I should have taken one of the rifles and hidden it in the woods. I'd be able to go and collect it now. I would have had plenty of time.

The adults were out of the house all day, moving across the moor, going through thousands of rounds of ammunition. While they were gone, I played in the stream, which they called a burn, and which ran wide and shallow over pebbles, under a bridge with a double arch.

The adults didn't come back for lunch. One of the servants drove a small lorry over the hills to meet them with wicker baskets of cold chicken and lobster. From the stream, I watched the lorry rattle away over the rough ground, while the cold water swept around my ankles. I'd been gathering pebbles. I should have dropped them then, and climbed onto the bank, and walked back to the empty house and the gun room. I needed a rifle now, in Crail, because it wasn't over.

One day on that trip, it rained too hard for them to shoot. My father borrowed a jeep and the two of us drove across the moor to the loch. Rain flashed away from the windscreen wipers, and we had to shout to hear each other over it. My father told me that Sam's grandmother had said there was a monster in their loch. She'd swum near it once when she was a little girl. "Was she scared?" I asked.

"No, she said it was one of the best things that ever happened to her, she'd always wanted to see one."

"Has anyone else seen it?"

"Sam's uncle did. We can ask him about it at dinner tonight."

The jeep bounced on the rocks and scraped through the gorse. Ahead of us, the loch lay under dark mountains. As we drove around it, I watched its surface for the monster. Part of the track had been washed away. "Is it safe?" I asked.

"We'll be fine," he said. He often told me to worry less.

25

A LICE IS LYING on her stomach with her ankles crossed in the
air behind her. While we talk, she rubs the top of one foot
with the toes of the other. In front of us, women are standing on a
jetty, diving into the water, swimming across it. The trees around
the Kenwood Ladies' Pond are dense enough to hide it from view,
separating it from the rest of Hampstead Heath. I pull my wet
hair over my shoulder. Coming here was Alice's idea, she couldn't
believe I'd never been before.

On the slope above the pond, as our swimming costumes dry,
we've been talking about our ancestors. We both know a lot about
them. Alice's aunt is interested in genealogy, and I let her think
that my information comes from someone else in my family too,
that I wasn't the one who made an account on a heritage website
and paid to access the records.

I spent a while on it a few years ago. I copied down the family
tree on Mum's side, going back six generations, in careful, sepia

ink. I like to look at it and remind myself that I have parts of those people in me too, not only him.

"My great-grandmother was estranged from her siblings," says Alice, her arms bent behind her, tightening the straps of her bikini.

"Why?"

"There were three children, and she was the youngest. When her older sister and brother were teenagers, they fell in love and eloped."

"*Together?*" I ask.

"Yes. They changed their names when they ran away, and were never found."

I lie with my chin on my hands, facing a bee clinging to a stalk of clover. A woman dives into the pond and yelps at the cold water, and Alice says, "It's not even bad now. My mum swam here through the winter when we lived in Hampstead."

I turn to look at her. The Frasers never lived in Hampstead, they've had the house in Sussex and the one in Chelsea since before she was born. "Where did your family live?"

"Flask Walk," she says. I twist a piece of grass around my finger and tug. Maybe I'm wrong, maybe they stayed here temporarily once.

"Has it been hard keeping it a secret?" she asks.

"Sorry?"

"From your parents," she says. "You must want to tell them about the party."

Across the pond, the wind parts the branches of a willow, showing the room inside. For the first time, I let myself imagine that I haven't lied to Alice, that my parents are happily married, that I am planning a surprise party for their anniversary. "It has been hard, I've almost mentioned it by accident a few times."

"Where were they married?" she asks, and her expression seems concentrated, harder than usual.

"A registry office. How long have your parents been married?"

"Thirty-five years," she says, then rolls onto her back and closes her eyes. I don't know what has just happened, if she's testing me. If she's about to ask the name of the registry office, if she's going to look at the records and find none with my surname. I try to remember if I made a mistake earlier, when we were talking about our ancestors, but I only told her vague details, not any of their names.

Alice seems to fall asleep. I look at the row of orange life preservers and try to think of how to answer the different questions she might ask. Eventually, she sits up. "Ready?"

We walk down the heath, which is green and rippling with shadows from the few high clouds, the birds, and us. I still can't tell if she was baiting me earlier, or if now she seems quieter than usual. Alice takes out a bag of Maltesers and eats them while we walk. We're crossing a hollow near Pryor's Field when I hear a sound, like a gurgle, and Alice stops short. She drops the bag of chocolates and holds her hands to her throat as her eyes widen.

I step behind her, put my arms around her torso, and drive my fist into her diaphragm. Her body jolts against mine. I do it again, harder, and she coughs the chocolate onto the grass.

She wheezes, bent over, her hands on her chest. We're alone, no one saw it happen, or is coming to ask if we're all right. Alice has started to laugh, hysterically, and I drop onto the grass. Around us, the full green trees move in the wind.

"Oh," she says, "you're crying."

I wipe my eyes with my sleeve. She sits next to me, puts her arm around me, and says, "Thank you, Claire." When my knees stop knocking together, we continue on, still arm in arm. Alice tells me what it felt like, what she thought was going to happen. She must find my response odd for a doctor, but I can't explain it to her. When she choked, I hadn't knocked into her, I didn't push her, but it still feels like my fault, like I wished for this to happen since now she's in my debt.

26

MUM WAS IN the garden chopping wood. Sunlight swept down the blade as the axe fell; she must have oiled it recently. The log split and its halves dropped into the snow. When she finished, she left the axe wedged into the trunk, its red handle in the air, which was a stupid thing to do, anyone could come and take it. I went down to the garden and replaced the axe in the shed.

That night, Mum made a fire with the wood she'd chopped. I looked at the logs and thought, I'll wait until that one catches, then I'll ask her. She was still kneeling by the fire, and small twists of burnt paper sailed up the chimney.

"Why did he do it?" I asked. After staring into the fire, Mum had to blink to see me.

"I don't know," she said. I'd asked her before, and this had been her answer then too. The air above the fire wavered with heat.

"Did he think you were going to take his money?"

"No, most of his money was in trusts, they're protected in a divorce."

"What about the house?"

"I didn't want us to live in that house," she said. "I was about to put down the deposit on a place in Highbury." This news upset me, like we'd almost escaped in time.

"Had he met someone else?"

"We were separated," she said crisply. "That wouldn't have been a problem."

"Was he worried about his reputation?"

"What do you mean?" she asked, turning towards me. With her broad mouth and deep-set eyes, she looked so little like the woman in the old pictures. Behind her, one of the logs collapsed in the grate.

"With the divorce. Did he think you'd say things about him?" Mum shrugged. She reached her hand in to shift a log and pulled it out just ahead of a burst of sparks. I said, "You must have thought of something."

"He was angry with me," she said. "He seemed to think I was getting in his way."

"Why?"

"I don't know, Claire."

"In the way of what?" I asked, and she shook her head. "Why did his friends help him?"

"They'd known him for longer."

"What about Emma?"

"They didn't think about Emma."

I VISITED EMMA'S MUM, Nancy, in Birmingham eight years ago. On one of my days off from St George's, I took the train north, and a cab to her house in Balsall Heath.

I'd written to her first, she was expecting me. We sat in her front room and she told me how it had been for her. How it was still. I stayed motionless, pinned in place, while she talked, her eyes on the carpet.

She had separated from her husband, Emma's father, two years after their daughter died. She still saw Joe sometimes, and said they both hoped that one day it wouldn't be so painful for them to see each other, and that they would live together again.

They had scattered their daughter's ashes on a hill in France, near Aubrac, where they'd gone on holiday when Emma was seventeen.

"She was so taken with it," said Nancy. "She said it was the best place she'd ever seen."

Nancy showed me a picture of the monastery they'd visited where, during winter storms, the monks toll bells to guide anyone lost in the snow.

We went through albums with pictures of Emma. Nancy looked at me intently, and I wondered if she was trying to see him in my face.

"My mum loved Emma," I said. "She felt so guilty that it was Emma and not her."

"I know," said Nancy. "We wrote to each other."

I startled. "Did you?"

"I went over to her after the inquest, to tell her it wasn't her fault."

I started crying then. Nancy said, "We met a few times. At a tea shop near the train station in Edinburgh. What's its name?"

"Waverley Station."

"Yes," she said, "that's it."

27

T HE STILL LIFE shows oysters and lemons painted four hundred years ago in Holland, and I feel sorry for it having ended up here, in this room of braying people, and that one of them might take it home.

Alice hands me a glass of champagne, then stands at my shoulder to consider the painting. We've been spending a lot of time together in the past few weeks, since the afternoon on the heath. I still feel guilty, like I wished for her to almost die, and knew how much saving her would help me. It did change our friendship, almost instantly. We started talking on the phone, and seeing each other more often, and she's invited me out for hikes, dinners, films, and now this, a private view at Sotheby's.

We're in a room of Dutch still lifes that will be auctioned next week. I look at another painting, of frilled red tulips and a silver trout, and can't believe someone will be allowed to buy it. Alice points at the delicate wet scales on the fish. Behind us, a man is describing his birthday party. "The theme is younger sons," he says. "Each table will be named after a different famous younger son."

It's the end of August. I told Alice a few days ago that my father had broken his hip and I needed to cancel their party. She was disappointed for us, but told me that of course she wouldn't bill me for the event. She tried to return my deposit too, but I insisted that she keep it.

Alice is still absorbed by the painting. She's a good person to be with in a gallery, private and thoughtful, and seems unbothered by the people around us. I yawn, and consider leaving and coming back in the morning, when the gallery is open to the public and these people will be gone.

I was up in the night worrying about Robbie. And almost all of my patients today were difficult. One of them complained about the wait, and I couldn't tell her that I was late because the patient before her had told me he'd started self-harming with a straight razor.

I follow Alice into the next gallery, squeezing past a group in the doorway. At its centre, talking loudly, is Sam.

My pulse starts to thump all across my body, thick in my wrists and throat and the backs of my knees. The last time I saw Sam was three years ago, after the newspaper published the story about his house in Chelsea. He saw me too, across the road from his doorstep, he stopped and stared at me, a puzzled look on his face.

He's wearing yellow trousers with a white shirt tucked into them. His red hair has started to recede, and his brows are fair, so his forehead seems to jut unbroken over his eyes. His face looks old-fashioned, something about the light-blue eyes and the long space between his nose and mouth.

Sam holds his fist near his mouth while he swallows, so that no one else will start talking. The group waits until he clears his throat. "I came back from squash yesterday and couldn't walk, and just sat in front of the painting while I recovered." He starts to describe the still life he owns, by one of the Dutch masters whose work is for sale in this auction. I notice that his tongue is white, like he doesn't brush it. A woman says, "I think this era marks—"

Sam shouts, "Alice!" She smiles when she sees him. He puts his arm around her shoulders and turns her to face the group. "This is my goddaughter."

Alice says, "Have you met my friend Claire?"

Sam kisses me hello. As he moves to kiss the other cheek, I'm close enough to smell the whisky in his mouth. "Nice to meet you," I say. He looks me over, then returns to Alice. He hasn't recognized me. "What happened with your accountant?" he asks Alice.

"It's a disaster," she says.

"Right, let's get dinner this week, I want to hear about it," he says.

"Let's. Did you see they're serving your wine?" asks Alice. Sam owns a vineyard in Kent called Dionysius. He stops a server and asks her to fetch a bottle. The back of the label says, helpfully, that Dionysius is the Greek god of wine. He was also a tyrant who ruled Syracuse in ancient Greece and ordered hundreds of executions, which I stop myself mentioning.

"How're the vines?" asks Alice.

"Fine, fine, fully recovered," says Sam. To the group, he says,

"Four years ago, we had rot and lost the entire harvest." It's an effort not to smile, I hadn't known about that. He says, "You hear about industrial sabotage in France every few years."

"No one would do that to you," says Alice.

"Oh, I can think of a few people," says Sam, smiling. I heard he'd been in trouble at university. A girl made a complaint about him, though she withdrew it, and never went to the police.

I finish my champagne. Not a good idea, three glasses of it without any food. I look at the white lines across Sam's throat where the skin hasn't tanned. He's teasing Alice about one of the ushers at a wedding last month, and she rolls her eyes. The rest of the group realize they aren't going to be involved in the conversation and start to talk among themselves. There's a plastic stirrer in his drink. I saw them at the bar, they have sharp points. I could get it from his glass and slide it into his carotid artery.

It seems impossible that he hasn't sensed anything, that he thinks I'm a stranger. Finally, Sam looks at his watch. "I've got to run, I have a dinner at Rules."

Rules was my father's favourite restaurant. I had dinner there once as part of my research. It's the oldest restaurant in London. There were booths on thick carpets, oil paintings of game birds, and a waiter cutting slices of beef Wellington from a trolley. They served the same boarding-school desserts as Sweetings, and a lot of the guests seemed to know one another.

My father must miss it. Not just the restaurant, but its particular version of England. He must not like the food or the landscape as much wherever he is now. The thought makes me furious, that he might think he still deserves to have whatever he wants.

Alice and I move through the rest of the exhibit while Sam

heads down the road to Rules. Then what? 5 Hertford? A strip club? I can't picture him alone. I doubt he is often.

Everything would be different if Sam hadn't qualified for a pilot's licence. He kept a Cessna at a private airfield in Kent, and the night after the murder, he took it out for a flight. He told the police he'd only gone to Whitstable and back, but there was no warden at the airfield to confirm it, and no records of his flight path, since he flew so far below commercial airspace.

The police believe that Rose or James drove my father's car to Newhaven, while he hid at Ashdown. The next night, one of them drove him to the airfield in Kent and Sam flew him out of the country. To Germany, maybe, or Belgium.

The flight to Germany would have lasted ninety minutes. I want to know what they talked about. I think both of them would have taken pride in having a normal conversation in those circumstances, like it proved they were braver and steadier than other men.

My father once told me a story about an English pilot whose plane was shot down during the Battle of Britain. He bailed out with a parachute and landed in the Surrey countryside on the grounds of a lawn tennis club. The club offered him white flannels and a racquet, and invited him to play while he waited for the RAF van to come for him. The pilot beat everyone who played him. When my father told me the story, I pictured him as the pilot. I wonder if he did too.

After Sam left him, he must have hiked alone into the countryside. The experience might have felt familiar from all the accounts he'd read of men in the war, walking alone past farmhouses. He might have felt a comradeship with them. I wonder what he ate, where he slept. Those stories might have given him practical ideas. They might have prepared him to enjoy it.

28

I wait for Alice outside a small station in Sussex, with my bag at my feet and the bottle of wine I bought at Waterloo. A few days after the gallery event, she invited me to Ashdown for the weekend.

"Sorry I'm late," she says, coming to help carry my things. The air is cool here in the countryside, and she's wearing a blue-and-cream Fair Isle cardigan with wooden toggles.

I stow my book and follow her to the car. Stella barks from the back seat and I turn around to pet her. When Alice stops at a crossing, the sound of the indicator clicking fills the car. "Who else is at the house?" I ask.

"My parents, four of their friends, my cousins, and this man from work Mum invited by accident."

We drive past a herd of sheep painted with red marks. I wonder how long sheep live, if these are the descendants of the ones Mum saw when she came here.

The evening sky grows dark above the hedgerows. When we reach Maresfield, I look at the village sign and remember my father telling me that during the war it was painted over to confuse the Germans in a land invasion.

"Did Ashdown have evacuees during the war?" I ask.

Alice shakes her head. "Too near the coast, it wasn't safe enough." During the Blitz, my grandmother had children evacuated from London at her estate in Norfolk. She mentioned it often, as though it made up for all the years when the vast house didn't help anyone.

Alice turns onto Hindleap Lane. I remember this road, the dense woods around it, and the stone lions at the gate. The gate glides open, letting us through onto a long drive lined with poplars. Wind rushes through the trees, and in our headlights the shadows on the gravel blur and race and lengthen.

We come around a bend in the drive, and there is the house, a Palladian mansion, the stones stained grey with age. Night-time clouds race past its towering roof. My father must have been so relieved to arrive here that night, to watch the gates close behind him. Alice locks her car, and her body is lit red as the tail-lights flash.

When she opens the front door, two Rhodesian ridgebacks run towards us. The dogs have a bristling line of fur down their backs, so they always seem to have their hackles raised. Voices are coming from the drawing room. I want to pull on Alice's sleeve, ask her to wait a minute, but then we're inside and the group has encircled us. I meet her cousins Beatrice and Anna, an older man in tweeds, a woman with a German accent, and another cousin, Luke, who's just back from Vietnam. He has a red string tied around his wrist, from Vietnam, presumably.

James is on the sofa, with one ankle crossed on his knee and a stretch of ribbed yellow sock showing. "Dad, you remember Claire," says Alice. He rises from the sofa to kiss me as Rose appears at his side. "How nice to see you again," she says warmly, and I wonder if Alice told them about what happened on the heath.

All of the other guests have versions of the same accent, except for the woman from Berlin. Alice leads me to a corner of the room where a bar trolley is crowded with spirits, bitters, bourbon cherries. Rose gave my father brandy when he reached the house, to help with the shock. I lift the bottles, like I'll find that particular one.

I think Rose and James have been in touch with my father, and if they have, there has to be a trace of it somewhere in this house. A letter, or bill, or photograph, or note in a calendar. They wouldn't need to destroy those small pieces of evidence anymore, they aren't under investigation. I'm impatient to start looking, but it will be hours until everyone else goes to bed.

One of James's friends is also a doctor, and works at a clinic on Harley Street. "Have you considered switching to private?" he asks.

"No. I want to work for the NHS."

"Well, I'm glad someone does." He says it without malice, though, and he doesn't tell me how much more money I'd make.

At eight we move into the dining room and Rose directs everyone to a seat. I'm near the end between Luke and Alice. I've never eaten in this room before. All of the children ate near the nursery, though once, when I wasn't feeling well, I was allowed inside to sit on Mum's lap.

Two girls in blue linen shirts bring in bowls of risotto with wild mushrooms. While we eat, Luke tells me that he lives in Hanoi. Alice snorts. "You have a flat in Fulham."

To me, he says, "I'm back and forth a lot."

Our movements around the long table make the candlelight flicker on the ceiling and the walls. I look at a Tudor painting of a woman in a black dress and spiked lace collar, holding a rosary. Splinters of other conversations come down the table. "This was when we were at Cambridge."

"They're just back from Cortina."

"The Lion d'Or?"

"We're going to Rovinj."

"Where is that?"

"Croatia."

Alice looks at her parents. "You've been to Croatia, haven't you?" James shakes his head. "I thought you went after Greece, I thought you stayed in Skopje."

"That's in Macedonia. We went to Macedonia after Greece."

Luke answers my questions about his job and his travels at length, which means I can mostly listen to the other conversations. After dessert, slices of chocolate ganache tart, we leave our plates on the table. A few of the guests go onto the terrace to smoke and the rest of us move to the drawing room.

"My phone's not working," says Beatrice.

"There's no signal," says Rose. "We think there must be lead in the walls, nothing gets through."

There are twelve of us, a big enough group that I can recede without anyone noticing. They all have their own concerns, anyway. One couple isn't getting along very well, and the man from

Rose's office is drinking much faster than any of the others. I wonder if he's realized he wasn't meant to be invited.

And James doesn't seem to want guests at all. Whenever he can, he busies himself with small tasks, separate from the others, like fixing the wobbly leg on the bar trolley. At dinner I catch him reading the label on the back of a bottle of wine. He's affectionate with Rose, though. I think he'd rather be alone here with her and their daughter, which is a shame. If they hated each other, one of them might tell me what the other had done.

Someone came into my bedroom during dinner to draw the curtains and close the wooden shutters. I pull them open again and watch the moon reeling behind the clouds. I've never stayed anywhere so quiet before. In my flat, I can hear radiators hissing, pipes clicking, my neighbours' voices, car alarms. The water and heat and electricity here are all somehow silent.

I wish I could have brought Jasper instead of leaving him with Laila for the weekend, and thinking of him makes me homesick, like I've been away for months.

I wait for a few hours, then softly open my door. The corridor is so long that if someone were standing at its far end, I wouldn't be able to see his face. I listen from the top of the stairs. The wind against the house, nothing else. It's three in the morning now, everyone must be asleep. I won't have much time. James wakes at five during the week, he might keep the same schedule here.

On the ground floor, I remember from our visits that the kitchen wing is to the left, and an office is somewhere to the right.

I open six doors before finding it, a small room near the west end of the house. On the walls are framed landscape plans and a shelf of farming almanacs. The desk is covered with papers, books, and a stuffed partridge under a glass bell.

I start to sort through the papers, but all of them have to do with the house. They're bills for repairs on the chimney, maintenance on the tennis court, an estimate for replacing a section of roof damaged in a storm. It's an estate office. Rose and James might never come into this room, none of the papers have their signatures, only the estate manager's.

I leave the office and move from west to east, opening doors, searching for box files, a planner, an address book. In the library, I find a few envelopes and scraps of paper stuck between the books, but none of them are useful, and already it's almost five.

In the morning, sheep move through a thick fog on the lawns around the house. I watch them while dressing in a loose cashmere jumper, jeans, and moccasins. Normal, a normal houseguest. Someone has set coffee, bread and fruit on the dining table, though the house is quiet, the drawing room empty. I step onto the terrace. James is coming up the slope of the lawn in a green waxed jacket. His face is pinched and white from the cold, but he looks happier than he did last night. "Morning," I say, as he climbs the steps, stripping off a pair of work gloves. "Have you been in the garden already?"

"Yes. Stay away from gardening, it's a thankless job."

"Can I see it?" He seems to consider pointing me towards it, then steels himself and leads me down the slope. He says, "It might hail tonight. Not the September weather we expected, unfortunately." He doesn't sound disappointed.

"Still gorgeous," I say.

"Yes," he says, with feeling. We step into the walled garden, where quinces, plums and pears hang from branches. James notices me looking at the holes in the brick walls. "They're fireplaces," he says, "though we don't use them. Winters aren't as cold anymore."

I remember curling into one of the spaces, Mum coming to find me, saying, There you are! I have to force myself to turn away.

James stands with his shoulders hunched and his hands in his pockets. He's different than he was at forty. He's different even than he was nine years ago, when I followed him. He was more confident then, he didn't have this current of unease, and I wonder what happened to change him.

After he shows me the stables, we walk to the edge of the property, to a stone church surrounded by hemlocks. Rows of gravestones rise in the tall grass. "Whose are they?" I ask.

"My family," he says, switching a stick through the grass, then realizes this sounds cavalier, and says, "Distant ones. None I ever met."

I count eight graves. "When was the last person buried here?"

"Nineteen fifty-four," he says. "My great-uncle." We stand for a moment looking at the worn stones under the hemlocks.

There was a rumour that my father never left their property that night, that one of his friends shot him and they buried him in one of these graves. It's never seemed likely, they didn't have a motive.

The ground is raised in places where the land has settled, so it looks as though the coffins are pressing from under the earth. Apparently it's the best place to hide a body, in an existing coffin. No one wants to disturb a grave.

We climb the hill to the house, where Alice's cousins are smoking on the terrace in their pyjamas. The girls stretch and yawn. Beatrice rubs her eyes, and Anna looks me up and down. "You look nice."

The others are inside having breakfast, and I pour myself a coffee and take a piece of soda bread, though my appetite's gone. Luke crunches toast while reading the memoir of a man who founded a nonprofit in Nepal. Rose turns over the newspaper with a sound of disgust. "I can't look at him."

After a pause, Luke says, "Aren't you used to that sort of thing?"

"What do you mean?"

"You're a barrister."

"Corporate. Not criminal."

A heavy rain starts to fall. Through the open doorway and the wide stairwell, we can hear it thundering on the roof. "It could be like this for forty-eight hours," says the man from Rose's office, eagerly.

Later in the morning, I return to the dining room, but the table's been cleared. I search downstairs until I find a basket of newspapers next to the fireplace in the library, and sift through it for the one Rose was reading. On the front page is a picture of a man in Bristol who murdered two children. I sit there for a long time, looking at his face.

There's a photograph of Rose on the mantel. It was taken years ago, she can't be much older than thirty. She's leaning against a stone wall somewhere, with her arms behind her back. I look at that for a long time too.

One of their neighbours said he heard a gunshot the night my father came here. A few hours later, at dawn, the neighbour went into the woods with his dog, and part of his route took him by the fence around Ashdown. He told the police he saw a man walking up the slope from the churchyard, between the hemlocks. The light wasn't good, it was still early in the morning, but he said the man was holding a shovel.

In the servants' wing, the floors and walls are stone, the ceiling is low, and the air is much colder than in the rest of the house. Where the corridor splits, I remember that one way leads to the gun room and the other to the kitchen.

The kitchen has a vaulted ceiling, with ribs, like a cathedral. It's large enough to feel empty, even though there are two vast ovens, a deep soapstone sink, and long counters. One wall is covered by a mechanism of iron rods and gears, a roasting spit, large enough to cook huge sides of meat. A charnel smell rises from the iron. Footsteps come down the hall, and I hurry through the scullery and out a side door onto the lawn.

You can't see the church from the house. It's down a slope at the edge of the property, hidden by the hemlocks. I can't remember if James was more uneasy in the churchyard than in the garden, he seemed discomfited the entire time.

My father arrived at their house at eleven thirty that night, and no one ever saw him again. How can that be possible, with a search that size, with his picture in all the newspapers. He might have never left the Frasers' property. Sam's flight the following night might have been a coincidence, he might have told the truth about only going to Whitstable.

I've never considered the possibility seriously before. But it seems more likely now, when decades have passed, when search methods have improved so much, and still he's never been found.

James is hitting golf balls from the top of the lawn in the rain. He raises the club over his head, then pauses before bringing it down. There's a crack and the ball whips into the distance. The rain makes it difficult to see where it lands.

I'm reading in the drawing room, with Alice at the other end of the sofa. She's meant to be working on new menu ideas, though she hasn't written anything down in a while. Rain streaks the windows, and a crack comes from outside every time James's club hits the ball.

Golf was a Ramsden Club tradition. Another tradition was that once a year they dressed in tailcoats and drove out of Oxford to a country pub. They posed for a photograph in front of the pub, a group of eight handsome young men.

They rented a room at the pub, the sort normally used for leaving dos or special anniversaries. They had a long meal and drank wine. They were impeccably polite to the servers, and pretended to be enthusiastic about the food.

Then, before they left, they smashed the room to pieces. Broke all the furniture, tore the paper from the walls, stamped on the glasses.

They offered the owner of the pub a huge, absurd sum of money to pay for the damages, more than would come from insurance or a court settlement. A few of the owners still called the police, but over the years most, by far, took the money. So it wasn't really about fun, or excess, or rioting, it was about humiliation.

None of them were punished. Our prime minister joined in the tradition, as did our foreign secretary, and my father, and his friends.

While everyone else is upstairs dressing for dinner, I walk to the gun room. The door is locked. I feel along the lintel for a key, and my hand comes away covered in dust. I press my face to the crack between the door and the frame, and see a cabinet with rows of upright rifles.

At dinner, we're served iced lobster soufflés and champagne. Everyone is talking even faster than last night, and I have to wait for a pause in the conversation before turning to Rose. "Do you have services at the church?"

"No," she says. They did before, I remember. There's a separate gate at that end of the property, and on Sunday morning it was opened to the locals. "Our congregation was combined with the one in Maresfield."

"When?"

"Years ago, early nineties."

After my father disappeared, then. The Frasers might not have wanted people on their property anymore, near the graveyard.

Maybe Rose refused to help my father, and he threatened her. They were best friends, he knew everything about her and James, he could have blackmailed them. He wouldn't need to know much. She's a barrister, even a small misconduct could destroy her.

They own rifles. Maybe she shot him, and James helped her bury the body in one of the graves. She drove the car to Newhaven and left it near a cliff so it would look like he'd committed suicide. She allowed the police to suspect that she'd helped my father escape, because that was better than if they suspected she'd killed him.

She could justify it to herself. She'd met Emma, and he had murdered her. She would be doing him a kindness, in a way.

Late in the night, I step outside, lifting the hood of my coat. A few of the others are still awake, I can hear them in the drawing room, but it's raining, no one will come outside. I walk to the edge of the property and climb down the slope, between the hemlocks, the wet grass sliding under my boots. I stand beside the church and look at the eight gravestones.

No one will be able to see me from the house. Beneath my feet the ground is soft and cushioned. My eyes have adjusted to the darkness and I can see the white spots on the oldest gravestones. This could all be over in a few hours. I saw where they keep the shovels.

I look down the path towards the woods. No one is coming to help. The police were told to look here and they didn't.

A few hours with the shovel, that's all. When it's over, I won't remember it. It will seem like a dream, it already does.

Rain slides from the hemlocks. I should have started by now. I won't be able to dig in the daylight, someone might come past. But my arms hang at my sides. I open and close my fists. I could be at a police station soon, warm and dry, while officers finish exhuming his body.

I walk around the church for the shovel. Maybe this will be easier once it's in my hand. I return to the graves, push the tip of the shovel into the dirt, and use my foot to drive the blade further into the ground. I wipe my dirty hand across my forehead and start to dig.

29

WE WERE DRIVING to the Highlands. I had the atlas open on my lap, even though Mum said she wouldn't need directions until after Inverness. We'd passed Dalwhinnie and were crossing the floor of a broad valley where the shadows of clouds moved over the hills and the moors.

I found our destination on the atlas. Glen Affric was on the other side of Loch Ness, in the northern Highlands. Mum had already told Robbie that a glen was a valley, and he said, "I know, we've done that." It was impossible to guess what Robbie had covered in school. His class had learned about Kepler's laws, for example, but not fractions.

Robbie was in the back seat, wedged in the small space left beside our bags and Finn, who was sitting up on a corduroy dog bed and looking out of the window. A few presents were hidden in the bags, it would be Christmas in three days. Mum's friend from work had loaned her his cottage for the holiday. The drive would take around four and a half hours. Already the landscape had started to change, and I was eager to travel farther north, to put more distance between myself and school. My exams hadn't gone well. I'd been staying up late to read about my father, and hadn't been able to concentrate on the test questions. Thinking about them made me feel sick.

Mum flailed her arm towards the back seat. "What do you need?" I asked.

"Crisps." I opened the bag and held it towards her. She was wearing an old fleece and a thick wool scarf. It would be colder in the north.

Alongside the road, the hills had the texture and colour of deer hide. My exams started to seem like less of a problem. I'd have to work harder next term to make up for them, but the holiday had just begun, that was still days away.

We crossed the suspension bridge over the Moray Firth, and I looked between its spans at the dark water flooding into the North Sea.

"You need the A832 now," I told Mum. Behind us, Robbie was reading a comic book, with one arm draped over the bags to rest on the dog.

The road narrowed, curving past farms and paddocks. We stopped in Cannich for supplies. "There won't be anything near the house," said Mum. We bought food, bottles of water, and a large box of matches for the hob.

The last stretch of the drive was on a single-track road along a river until we reached the house, an old cottage at the bottom of a mountain with spruces planted behind it to block the wind. Robbie and the dog spilled out of the car and ran to look at the river. Mum found the key under a stone, and we went inside.

We weren't completely alone in the glen, there was also a private estate, and an estate keeper's cottage. The estate house was on an island in the river at one end of a short, humpbacked wooden bridge. Smoke rose from its chimneys, someone was at home. "Who lives there?" I asked Mum, and she shrugged.

I could see two horses in a paddock by the estate keeper's cottage. No people, though. Mum said she doubted anyone lived here year-round, since the roads must often be blocked by snow. Which meant we could be snowed in, too. The cottage's power came from a generator. "What happens if it turns off?" I asked.

"It won't," said Mum.

The estate was doubled in the slow-moving river. Its witch's-hat turrets, chimneys, lines of smoke. We weren't very far from Sam's house in Inverness. These might be friends of his, all of the landowner families here seemed to know one another.

We unpacked the groceries from the car, the biscuits, milk, pasta, butter, tea. The cottage had a two-burner range. Mum held a match to the ticking gas and the flame caught. I said, "I'm going for a walk."

I started to climb the foothills behind the house. There was a path at first, then it disappeared and I scrabbled over the flattened brown grass and granite outcroppings. The wind had stopped and I was the only thing on the hill making any sounds.

This walk was a test, like the ones I'd begun setting for myself at home in Crail: walking back from Nell's alone at night, going down into the cellar, having a shower when no one else was home. I'd tried to have a bath, which hadn't worked, my heart was beating hard enough to make the surface of the water pulse. I'd try again when we returned home. I needed to practise that sort of thing now, or I'd never be able to go away to university, or ever live on my own.

The cottage grew smaller below me. Mum and Robbie were inside, they wouldn't be able to hear anything from up here. I reached the top of the first slope, a flat, bare stretch before another, steeper climb. Black streams branched through the peat, and their sound made the hair stand up on the back of my neck.

From the base of the next slope, the river wasn't in view anymore, or the cottage, which meant no one there would be able to see me. I walked over the trampled grass and around the rocks. The walk wasn't really a test. For it to be a test, I'd need to think that this was only practice, that really I was safe. But I thought someone was going to follow me, and I wanted to get it over with. I didn't know what I imagined would happen exactly, but I'd brought a knife in my pocket, in case. I thought that whatever happened, at least I wouldn't be scared afterwards, that this part would have ended.

The climb down was faster. A thin layer of cloud had covered the sky and the air had grown colder. Below me, wind brushed the river silver, and the two horses moved around the paddock. Someone had put blankets on them while I was gone.

It was stupid to be disappointed. Of course I'd rather be climbing back down, instead of being up on the hillside with someone who had followed me.

When I reached the cottage, Mum and Robbie looked up from their card game. "How was your walk?"

"Fine." In the kitchen, I tried to replace the knife in its drawer without a sound.

At night, the valley turned completely black, except for the lit windows in the estate house on the island in the river. I watched the windows but no one went past them. "Have you seen anyone there yet?" I asked.

"No," said Mum, without looking up from her book. I didn't understand why she wasn't worried. Whoever they were, they were the only other people for miles.

On the hill the next afternoon, we stopped so Mum could catch her breath. Below us, the river curved between the moors and stands of dark pines. Mum rubbed at her chest with a gloved hand. I shifted my weight and felt the peat sink under my boots. Robbie pointed at a herd of red deer on one of the sloped moors below us. From this distance, they seemed to be climbing with odd, disjointed gaits.

We kept walking. Around us, the hillside rippled as the sun went in and out of clouds. After another hour, we stopped for bread and cheese, and cold slices of the apple pie we'd bought at the store in Cannich.

I opened the flask of water, its clasp falling against the tin with a satisfying clink. Mum brought me here on purpose, I thought. She knows I'm teetering and she wants me to come down on the side of travel, independence, bravery. This annoyed me. She couldn't tell me that I'd be safe. She had no idea if I would be or not. Though

I could see her point, the glen's point. I didn't want to never travel because it might mean being alone on a road at night, or taking a cab with a male driver.

From the ridge, we surveyed the lowlands and foothills and peaks. It would have been a shame not to see this. The estate house, far below us, was also beautiful. The people staying inside it didn't want to hurt us. They were here for the same reason we were, probably. If we came across them on the hill, they would smile and say hello. They wouldn't block our way, or drag us off the path.

My father, and his friends, and the men from the forum were only a few people. I shouldn't think of them.

I should think instead about the strangers in the Blacksmith's Arms that night, when Mum stumbled inside in her stockings, washed in blood. There were three people inside the pub, two customers and a woman behind the bar. She ran to Mum and eased her to the floor. She stripped off her cardigan and held it to the cut on Mum's stomach, which might have saved her life, she might have bled to death otherwise.

The two men ran to our house. They weren't armed, they didn't know if the person who'd attacked Mum was still inside, but they went anyway. One of them ran upstairs and lifted Robbie from his crib, the other found me hiding behind a chair. He picked me up and said, "It's all right, love, you're safe." His hand at the back of my head, his body hunched around mine like a shield as he carried me out of the house.

We finished the last of the cheddar and the apple pie and continued along the mountain. I started to think about what I needed to do to grow up into that sort of person, the sort of person who runs to help.

WE CAME BACK to Crail the day before New Year's. I spent New Year's Eve at the Vix with Nell, and the next day, we went to the East Neuk Hotel with our families for Hogmanay lunch. Nell's mum teased us, offering us haggis, saying we looked green.

School started again. I had not, at all, done well in my exams. A few of my teachers asked to speak to me, one asked if anything was the matter at home. She said I'd seemed distracted recently, and I promised to work harder this term. I hadn't visited the websites about my father since coming back from Glen Affric, I'd decided I was finished with it. I was still grinding my teeth, though. I started sleeping with a mouth guard that Mum and I bought at a sports shop in St Andrews, but I couldn't tell if it was helping.

ON THE LAST DAY of January, I rode the bus home from school with Nell. A lorry had broken down on the Anstruther Road, so the traffic narrowed into a single lane, and the ride took ten minutes longer than usual.

I said goodbye to Nell on the high street and turned towards Nethergate. The air was cold and windless. I had two school assignments to complete, and a magazine to read if I finished my work, and was so preoccupied that I took out my key before I noticed that our front door was hanging open.

There was dirt on the floor inside. It looked like part of a bootprint.

I'd gone through this in my head so many times. Don't make a sound, run to the high street, don't hesitate or look behind you until you're with other people. I was stumbling backwards when I noticed Mum's handbag, down the hall, on the table in the kitchen. She was inside.

I lifted the iron poker from the stand next to the fireplace. I left the front door open behind me, so a neighbour would hear if I screamed. Mum's keys were next to the handbag and her shoes were on the floor under the table. I held the poker in front of me with both hands, hard enough to cut lines into my palms, and went upstairs. She wasn't there, though, or in the garden.

I stood on our front path. The terraced houses across the road all looked empty, and the trees were upright in the still air. I could hear my breathing in the quiet. A door across the road was opening, and our neighbour Fiona was coming outside, without a coat. She ran towards me and my legs went soft.

"Where's my mum?" I asked, in a high, stretched voice.

"She had a heart attack."

I smiled at Fiona then. Holding my hand at my forehead, my eyes wet. No one had taken her, hurt her.

"Can you drive me to the hospital?" I asked.

"No, Claire," she said, and her voice broke. "She's not there. I'm so sorry."

My knees gave out then. Fiona tried to keep me upright but I fell onto the path. I was gasping, and trying to crawl on my hands and knees towards the house as she held me to her.

———

A Double Life

MUM WAS FORTY-FOUR when she had the heart attack. She'd had angina. I'd known that it was why she often had to catch her breath, and that it was a kind of heart disease, but not that it was dangerous. "There are two types," she'd told me. "I don't have the bad one."

I understand that heart attacks are common. But she was forty-four. She ate well. She didn't drink much, and she'd never smoked. She hated jogging, but liked to walk for hours on the coast path. Her family didn't have a history of heart disease.

Mum hadn't always had high blood pressure. Sabrina told me that she'd first started noticing the breathlessness and tightness in her chest the summer after the inquest. She developed it because of stress.

———

AFTER MUM DIED, Sabrina adopted us. She was living with her sons in Wales then, in Abergavenny, which is a perfectly nice town, and a place I never want to see again in my life.

Sabrina put two single beds in what had been a den. She bought new sheets and hung fairy lights around the window. I think about that often now, about her shopping for the sheets, and assembling the beds, and hanging the lights. I wasn't in a state then to notice the kindness.

She has always been kind to us, even in the beginning, when I was not at all easy to live with, when I didn't think I was going to survive it. Sabrina is loving, but sometimes that seems worse, like it only shows the gap between how she loves us and how she loves her own children, how Mum loved us.

30

"Is he still training to swim the Channel?" asks Rose at breakfast.

"No, that's finished," says Beatrice. "He's doing some mountaineering thing now. Is it Kilimanjaro?"

I don't know who they're talking about. Nor do I care. I scrape butter onto my toast while rain dashes against the windows. I haven't slept. At six in the morning, I rubbed concealer onto the red marks on my face where I'd raked at the skin.

I didn't search the churchyard last night. It was too much. I couldn't disinter a coffin, his or anyone else's. I only lifted a few heaps of dirt before I gave up, cleaned the shovel blade with my sleeve, and replaced it on the nail, then washed the mud from my clothes in the bathroom sink and lay awake until morning.

I try to put down my cup without rattling the saucer. I swallow my toast and listen, waiting for them to run out of people to discuss. "He's dug under his basement," says Luke. "He has four thousand square feet down there that no one knows about."

This will never work. Even years from now, they won't talk about my father in front of me. I'll still be sitting here, listening to them gossip.

There is a more direct route. I could find instructions online for how to load a rifle and turn off the safety. They keep ammunition in the gun room, I saw boxes of cartridges under the table. The door's locked but with an antique bolt, like the one in my room. It wouldn't be difficult to break. James is often alone in his study. I could close the door behind me, point the rifle at him, and say, Tell me where he is.

Across the table, James is eating black pudding, made from his own sheep, he told us. He's silent and preoccupied, with work, maybe, or the garden, or one of his other hobbies. Alice mentioned that he likes foraging for mushrooms. He has special equipment for it, apparently.

I wonder what Rose and James would say if they knew Mum had a heart attack. That her heart failed after years of heavy stress. I wonder if they would remember every time they'd called her a bitch and a liar, every time they'd accused her of framing my father, every time they'd said she was an unfit mother, and if they'd feel remorse. I want them to know what they did, and the effort of not telling them, right now, is making my teeth grate.

Rose has gone for a hack. She invited me and I said I didn't know how, which isn't strictly true. I learned in Norfolk when I was six, my father put me in a helmet and led me around the paddock on one of my grandmother's ponies.

I watch Rose in a hooded rain cape and the horse until they disappear into the woods. James is outside too, in the garden, and Alice is playing pool with her cousins. I climb the stairs to their bedroom.

James's study is off the master bedroom. It has a large desk with a view over the lawn, and walls lined with filing cabinets. I start to search for their telephone records, flipping through folders of medical paperwork, the bill for an outpatient visit to a clinic on Great Portland Street, an appointment reminder for a root canal, then through insurance and maintenance forms for their cars.

The third filing cabinet has their credit card statements. The folders are thick, since they have so many transactions every day. I read down the account summary, a list of payments at clothing shops, restaurants, hotels, petrol stations, dry cleaners, though I don't know what to look for in it.

They might not be in touch with my father at all. He might have never left their house that night. I'm here because I'm a coward, and this is easier than digging in the graveyard.

Someone coughs in the hallway, and I slide the cabinet closed. I reach the master bedroom just as Alice steps inside. She startles, lifting a hand to her chest. "Have you seen the dogs?" I say. "I heard them barking, are they stuck somewhere back here?"

"Dad took them outside."

"Oh, it must have been coming from there."

Alice nods, then turns away from me to open her mum's jewellery box.

*

I haven't left the house all day, and by dinner it's started to seem unreal. The candlelight is playing tricks, too. From the corner of my eye, the woman in the Tudor painting seems to be opening her mouth.

I don't think I can stay in this chair, in this room, for another minute, but we still have the main course ahead of us, and dessert. By the time bowls of panna cotta arrive, I'm a little drunk, and my ankles hurt from twisting my feet under the table, it's the only way I've been able to keep the rest of my body still.

"When is Phoebe's wedding?" asks Alice.

"They're not getting married," says Beatrice. "She ended it."

"Did she? Why?"

"She found out what he did on his stag night." There were other conversations down the table, but now everyone stops to listen. "His friends took him to Amsterdam," says Beatrice. "They went to the red-light district, and he chose one of the girls in the windows."

I look across to James. Under the table, my feet stop moving, and I carefully set down my spoon. James is listening with his chin on his hand, and a bemused expression.

He is trying to look normal. He's making an effort, which he never does, he's always remote at meals, staring into the middle distance, fidgeting.

Beatrice takes her time with the story. At one point, James crosses his arms over his chest and leans back in his chair, still turned towards her with a half-smile. I've never seen him like this before. His expression is benign, like he's humouring her by listening, like this has nothing to do with him, and doesn't make him uncomfortable.

After dinner, Alice begins to divide teams for Pictionary. I say I'm not feeling well, and return to my room. I sit cross-legged on the bed and open my laptop. This afternoon, I didn't try to look for proof that James visits prostitutes. There didn't seem to be any point—he'd pay for it in cash, and he withdrew money often enough to hide those transactions. But I'm not the first to wonder about this. I type, "How can I tell if my husband pays for sex?"

The first result is a thread on a forum for mothers. The post's author said she'd found some suspicious texts on her husband's phone, and asked, "Does this sound to you like he's meeting prostitutes?"

A few of the women who responded said that the same thing had happened to them. Most of their advice involved his phone, and sending baiting messages to the numbers, which wouldn't help me, since James must have a password on his.

"Do you have access to his bank statements?" wrote one. I reach over to the nightstand for a pen. "Has he made payments for hotel assistants, airport assistants, or massage services? Or reserved hotel rooms?" I'd noticed a few charges at London hotels, the Savoy and Claridge's, on their statements, but they could have been for client dinners or drinks, or renting conference rooms.

The next one wrote, "Look in his statements for 'AWork', it's a booking site." Another said to search his car for condoms, either new ones or scraps of foil from the wrappers, but I can't imagine he'd be that careless.

I read down the thread as the first woman debates what to do, regrets having found anything, worries about her children. It's so wrenching to read that I forget for a moment about my own research.

Afterwards, I can't sleep. Cold air seeps through a crack in the window, and I lie awake wondering how fastidious James has been.

"There's a point-to-point today," says Alice at breakfast. "Shall we go?"

"What's a point-to-point?" asks the man from Rose's office.

"It's like a steeplechase," she says, which doesn't really clarify things.

"Where?" asks James.

"Tonbridge."

"We'd have to leave soon," he says. James likes betting. The most surprising thing when I followed him was that he went to the dog tracks. He seemed to take a lot of pleasure in it, in filling out his cards and watching the greyhounds, and he was good at it, he often stopped at the desk to collect winnings.

Beatrice looks up from her phone. "Let's go," she says, envisioning the cider tent, no doubt, and running into people she knows.

"Mum?" asks Alice.

"You go," says Rose. "It's supposed to rain again."

"They have tents," says Alice. "And we can take umbrellas. Please?"

I wait, holding my breath, until Rose says, "Fine." There's a rush from the table and through the house. James leaves first, without waiting for any passengers, because he wants time to place his bets. Anna and Beatrice put on tight dresses and waxed rain jackets. I stop Alice in the hallway. "I think I'm coming down with something, maybe I shouldn't be out in the cold today."

"Do you want me to stay with you?"

"No, it's fine. I have some messages to catch up on for work anyway."

"Help yourself to anything in the kitchen," she says. "We should be back around four."

I watch their cars leave on the security monitor in the front hall, then climb the stairs to the study. James has been in the room since yesterday. The chair and telescope have been moved, and on the desk a gardening manual is open to a section on drainage.

I find the filing cabinet with his credit card statements and use my phone to photograph the pages. I have to work quickly, there are hundreds of sheets, dating back three years. The process becomes automatic. While taking each picture, I scan the list of transactions. The names of a few spas and massage parlours keep appearing, I should check if any of them has been under investigation.

The sound of a hoover stops in the hall, and one of the house-keepers knocks on the door to their bedroom. She tries to open it, but I've wedged a chair under the handle. After a moment, I hear her leave, and open the next folder.

When I finish the last statement, I check that the cabinets are closed, that his chair and book are in the correct position. I start going through the images in the corridor before I've even reached my room.

After three hours, my battery dies, and I have to stand to look for the charger. Pins and needles burst down my legs, I haven't moved from my position.

This isn't going to work. He's been too careful. There are no payments to hotel assistants, airport assistants, or massage services. I've looked up every spa that's appeared so far, and all of them seem reputable.

The next step will be to go through the payments to London hotels and see if any of them are the cost of a room for the night. Even if I learn that James booked a night at a hotel in London, though, that doesn't prove what he did in it.

I carry my phone to the wingback chair by the window. It begins to rain, which is unlucky, they might decide to come home early. I read down the payments from last April. They were in France for half the month, it seems. I start to skim more quickly, and then I see a payment, on the twenty-second of April, for thirty pounds, to AWork.

I tip my head back and close my eyes.

James visited the site the day they returned from holiday, which seems like cruel timing. He might have paid to view an escort's private gallery or to contact her. Two days later, there is a payment for £340 to Mayfair Health. I type in the name, and find a simple website, one page, with a telephone number. I practise first, until my voice sounds easy, cool, entitled.

"I want to book an appointment for my boyfriend's birthday," I say when a woman answers. "We've never done this before, can you tell me what to expect?"

James won three hundred pounds at the point-to-point. I hear about it in the front hall as they strip off their wet coats. Then they all disperse into the house, to shower, pack, find something to eat, and I stand alone in the hall, under the tapestry. It's a battle scene, though so faded you can barely see the figures.

"Alice," I say. "Will you go for a walk with me?"

"Isn't it raining?"

"No, not anymore."

"I was going to have a bath," she says.

"Please?"

She seems about to say something, then pulls on her coat. We cross the terrace and walk down the lawn, with the house's bulk behind us. The other guests must be getting ready to leave. It's dusk, and all of the property is in charcoal. We're out of sight of the house now, near the church.

"I have to tell you something," I say. Alice looks at me with a clear, poised face, and I think that she knows. She's known since the beginning, I was right about her testing me that day in Hampstead. She used the point-to-point as an excuse to help me, so I'd be alone in the house.

"I'm so sorry for lying." I expect Alice to interrupt me, to say that I don't need to explain, that she guessed months ago. But she's gone still, and her head is cocked to the side. My throat starts to close. "We met when we were children."

Alice has her arms crossed, and she looks disappointed now, irritated, like she wants to be finished with me, done with this, whatever it is.

I can't say it directly, the words won't form, so instead I say, "I've been here before. The last time was on Boxing Day, when I was eight and you were—"

Her head snaps upright. "Lydia?" she says.

I nod, even though no one except my brother has called me by the name in years.

"What are you doing here?" she asks. "What have you been doing?"

"I need your help."

She laughs. It's grown darker, I'm having trouble seeing her face. It strikes me that this is a terrible place for our conversation, in the cold and the damp, that it might make her feel threatened. I hadn't thought of it, I'd only been worried about someone overhearing us.

"I want to find my father," I say, and my voice sounds hollow, though I'm still hopeful. Alice is kind and thoughtful. She knows what happened to Emma and my mum.

"Stay away from me," she says.

"I just want to talk to him."

"I'm nothing to do with this. My parents are nothing to do with this."

"No, I don't want to involve them."

"They almost went to prison because of your mum," she says.

"Please, Alice, it's a small thing, it wouldn't take you much time." She starts to walk away from me, climbing the slope towards the hemlocks. To her back, I say, "You have to help me."

"Go home."

"I know something about your family."

She turns, shaking her head. "You're embarrassing yourself."

"I don't want to tell you," I say, and she keeps walking. "Please just help me." She slips a little on the wet grass, then catches her balance. I follow her. We pass between the hemlocks and the house appears in front of us, vast and solid, with tiles of lit windows. "Your father hires prostitutes."

Alice sighs. "No. I'm sorry, but no, he doesn't."

I hold out my phone. "Do you want to call her?"

She's started to cry. "Bitch."

Afterwards, I call a taxi to the station. Alice waits with me outside the house. Neither of us says anything. We haven't spoken since I explained what I want her to do now.

The taxi is coming up the drive. The headlights appear first, raking the side of the house, then us.

We don't say goodbye. When I turn around in my seat, Alice is still standing on the gravel with the house above her, and her expression is taut and stricken. Then she and the house are gone, and we're driving down the hill and through the gate.

31

I WONDER IF MUM would be ashamed of me. Alice will do what I asked, because she doesn't want her mum to learn that her husband visits escorts. Her mum who, this year, had breast cancer.

I wince, and settle on the floor next to Jasper. He's asleep, making soft, hushing sounds, and I lie with my head on his chest. I stay there for a long time, like being near the dog will make me good again, will clear away what I've done.

Alice is going to ask Sam where my father is living now. She's going to tell him that she can't ask her parents without worrying them, but has always been curious. He'll enjoy it, I think, being the one to tell her, to initiate her into the secret. He's less discreet than her parents.

"Why don't you ask my dad yourself?" she asked.

"He might warn my father," I said. "If you ask Sam, no one will suspect anything."

She's supposed to be meeting Sam for dinner next week. I don't know if this will work. Alice might tell her parents about me, though I doubt it, I think she'd be too embarrassed to confront her father, and she'd want to protect her mum. She'll want this to go away, to pretend it never happened.

———————

I HAD A PLAN for how to cope with the waiting. During the day I'd be busy with work, and afterwards I'd meet friends at restaurants or go to see a film every night until Alice and Sam's dinner. But Robbie had another seizure. He was unconscious for four minutes, and his convulsions tore muscles in his back.

Every night after work, I take the tube to the Royal Free to see him. He's on an antipsychotic for the withdrawal, and a sleeping medication. The doses seem to be stronger than last time. He's foggy, not himself, and I leave every visit stunned.

———————

I'M WAITING on the tube platform at Belsize Park when Alice sends me a text. It says, "Hvar Town, Croatia."

My first thought on the platform, with the phone in my hand, is of Emma. And how unfair it is that he's alive, that he's been alive all these years, and she hasn't.

I never really knew Emma. I adored her, but I only knew the parts of her that she would allow an eight-year-old to see, which strikes me now as an immeasurable loss.

———————

A Double Life

AT THE HOSPITAL, I sit next to Robbie. I don't tell him about Ash-down, or what I learned. He's tired. When he goes to the bathroom, his back is hunched, and he has to hold on to the wall for balance. I'll do anything, I think. I'll do anything to make this stop.

PART THREE
SCOTLAND

32

I'VE SPENT a lot of time reading about war criminals. I wanted to know what people do, after they've done something terrible, how they spend their time. The ones who interested me the most had gone into hiding and lived in secret for years. One was a Nazi who moved to Ireland after the war. He bought a yellow house with gingerbread trim in the countryside and began to raise lambs.

I want to know what this man thought about while farming, how he felt when he remembered the things he'd done. It must have had some effect. A tormenting one, hopefully, but maybe not. Maybe having a hidden life gave his current one glamour, allowed him to take more pleasure in country life than he would have otherwise.

Another former Nazi in Ireland became a publisher of academic textbooks, and another joined a country club in Dublin.

I've read a lot about Radovan Karadži , who arranged the murders of thousands of Croat and Muslim civilians during the

Yugoslavia war. After the war, after The Hague indicted him for war crimes, he disappeared. While in hiding, he published a book of poems under his real name. He also became a New Age healer. He performed acupuncture and became a specialist in sex therapy, helping couples trying to conceive. I wonder if it was a kind of joke on his part, or if he believed he had healing powers.

I won't need to read these case studies anymore. I won't have to guess at what my father has been doing, or who he has become, or what sort of house he lives in. I'm going to watch him, for my own sake, for the twenty-six years I've spent wondering, and then I'm going to call the police.

AT HEATHROW, I collect my ticket from the machine, pass through security, and walk to the gate. I've been in this terminal before. I've ordered a flat white at that café, bought magazines from that stand, watched the planes from that window, all of which seems strange now, like this time should be entirely different.

I try to call Robbie again as the other passengers line up to board, but he doesn't answer. We had an argument yesterday at his flat. He was sitting on his bed with his back against the wall while I pleaded with him to enter a detox. I said, "All I'm asking you to do is come downstairs with me and get in the car. You don't have to do anything else. Why is that so hard?"

"I can't."

"What about an outpatient detox? You can still sleep here." He shook his head. "Why not?"

"Don't shout at me," he said.

"I'm not shouting."

"Jesus. No wonder you're still single."

I laughed in surprise. It was good, though, I wanted him to be angry. "What about you, Robbie? When was your last girlfriend?"

We went off then, shouting at the top of our voices, until I realized that both of us wanted our mum to come in and tell us to stop fighting. I started to cry, and Robbie sat with his head down.

"I'm sorry," I said.

"Can you leave now?" he said. "I need to sleep."

I send him another message, then lift my bag and board the plane. I watch through the window until we're over the Adriatic. Every so often the clouds break and I can see container ships far below. I still can't believe that I am on a plane to the place where my father lives. The flight to Croatia is only three hours. He's only been three hours away, all this time.

At the gate, the other passengers click off their seat belts and open the overhead compartments. Two women in the aisle are speaking in Croat. I wonder if he's learned the language.

The line at passport control isn't very long. It's the middle of September now, past the high season. The official looks at me, then at my passport picture, and writes something on my embarkation card. I enter another room and speak with a different official, answering his questions carefully, presenting the address of my hotel in Hvar Town. I try to hide my delight. They don't think I look like my passport picture, it's worked.

After Alice sent me the text, I bought a ticket to Split. I asked Anton for leave to care for a family member. I've worked with him for seven years now, he trusts that I'd only ask in a crisis. I didn't say which family member, but he knows about Robbie and why I've had to miss work before. Anton said, "How long do you need? A month?"

Robbie is ill. I am taking care of him, in a way, but I'm still worried I'll be punished for the lie, that something will happen to him.

In the immigration room, the official studies my documents. After work yesterday, I stopped at a chemist's and bought a box of henna hair dye. At home, I put on the flimsy plastic gloves that came in the box, leaned over the sink, and squirted the dye into my hair, the smell of it burning in my nose. Jasper lifted his snout in the air, whined, and went into the bedroom. After rinsing out the dye, I dried my hair, then showered again. The colour's already started to fade and turn rusty from being washed.

Last week, as soon as I left Ashdown, I read interviews with actresses in which they described changing their appearance for a role, and made a list of the foods they ate to gain weight. At the supermarket, I filled a cart with cakes, crisps, doughnuts. These foods had the added benefit of making my skin break out, as the actresses had said they would.

I plucked my eyebrows, so they're quite thin now. I changed the parting in my hair and cut a sharper fringe. I looked at pictures of tourists and backpackers on islands in Croatia, then bought vests with lace trim, harem pants, cork sandals. I found a few photographs of myself as a child. My face was narrower, my features slighter. My hair was brown and much shorter, and I didn't have a fringe. My father won't recognize me. He might not have even without any of these preparations, he hasn't seen me since I was eight.

The official returns my documents and stamps my passport. I

smile at him and walk through the airport to the taxi rank. When we arrive at the terminal, the ferry to Hvar has just left. It's an island in a chain off the Dalmatian coast, I learned. A lot of tourists sail from island to island in the summer, the water is apparently very clear. Even here, in the crowded harbour, it's already clear, a striking greenish blue.

I buy a ticket and spend an hour waiting on a bench outside the ferry terminal. My bare arms start to redden in the sun. Two French backpackers stand near me. I'm dressed almost identically to the girl, in a tight top with thin straps, loose pants, and sandals, though she also has bracelets and a small silver toe ring.

When the next ferry arrives, the line of waiting cars switch on their engines and slowly drive on board. The ferry isn't full. One of the French backpackers stretches across a row of seats to sleep. An old Croatian couple divide the sections of a newspaper between them. I buy a burek, a filo pastry filled with cheese, and carry it onto the deck. The air smells of smoke and fuel. Below me, the metal ramp clanks each time another car drives onto the ferry. I look back at the tall limestone cliffs rising behind the coast, the Dinaric mountains. Villagers fled over them during the Mongol invasions, I read. A horn sounds, and the ferry pulls away from the dock. We'll be at Hvar in two hours.

As the ferry travels to sea, I watch the Dinaric mountains grow distant. They're vast enough that my father must be able to see them from the island.

He left England in November of 1991. At the time, Croatia was at war. It had declared independence from Yugoslavia that June and was fighting against the Yugoslav People's Army. Hundreds of thousands of civilians were fleeing the country. My father could move in the opposite direction, and no one would look for him. They wouldn't even think of it. The airports were closed, and there were no passenger flights into or out of the country, only UN and NATO ones. But there were gaps in the border, which he could have hiked across. It wouldn't have been hard to blend in, thousands of UN peacekeepers were sent to Croatia that year. My father would look like any of the other Europeans or Americans who had come to contain or profit from the war.

I think he would like living in a war zone. It would make him feel brave, without being in much danger. He could stay far from the worst of the fighting, he could move into one of the thousands of homes that had been abandoned.

Below me, a line of white foam furs along the hull of the ferry. We're far from the mainland now. Ahead of us are the first of the islands, Solta and Brac. I walk to the front of the boat as slowly the islands draw closer. They look improbable, like two sections of pine forest carved out and set on the sea. We pass between them and into the open water, the open Adriatic. Homer wrote about these islands. I wonder if that influenced my father's decision, he'd enjoyed studying Classics when he was at Eton.

But he might not be here, I repeat to myself as the ferry approaches the island. Alice or Sam might have lied, I shouldn't expect anything.

I don't believe it, though. After Alice texted me, I remembered that at dinner on my first night at Ashdown, Rose and James said they'd never been to Croatia. I went through the pictures I'd taken of their bank statements again and found a payment to a hotel in Dubrovnik.

And everything I've learned about this place would suit my

father, both his preferences and his unusual circumstances. Hvar is supposedly the most beautiful of the islands, and Hvar Town is where the wealthiest travellers visit. He'd be able to see the sort of people he likes.

The ferry docks at Stari Grad. When I climb down the rusty stairs, an attendant is directing a line of cars off the ferry. I follow a few of the other passengers to a bus stop, and set my bag in the dirt while searching through the unfamiliar banknotes for the fare.

A bus arrives, its exhaust sticking to the sweat on my face while I wait to board. The ride south across the island to Hvar Town will take twenty minutes. The bus is full, and I sit with my arms linked around my backpack. While researching Hvar and Croatia last night, I learned that thousands of UN peacekeepers and contractors stayed here after the war. Some of them became involved in the sex trade as clients. I don't know if that's the right word. The women weren't paid, and they couldn't leave. Some of the peacekeepers became traffickers themselves, of the women they had been trained and sent to protect. None of them have been arrested for this. None of them have been punished at all, as far as I know, though I hope I'm wrong, I hope someone has a list of those men and is working through them one by one.

The houses of Stari Grad fall away, and on either side of the road are rocky hills and low maritime trees. Late-afternoon sunlight slants through the olive bushes. Through the open window, I hear the bus tyres hiss on the tarmac. Ahead of us, the road curves between the limestone hills. The sun is low enough in the sky that some of the hillsides are in shadow and others are golden. We're in the island's interior now, but you can still tell that the sea is nearby. He's chosen such a beautiful place for himself.

I read that the hills are bare because medieval Venetians logged the island to build their ships. Hvar Town was a Venetian port once. He'd like that, he always liked Italy.

The road starts to drop down a hill. We pass a construction site behind a chain-link fence, a digger left beside a pile of rubble, then a few cement houses with bars over their windows. The road bends and Hvar Town appears below us, a jumble of red-tiled roofs on a slope around the harbour, the blue Adriatic stretching away to a line of haze at the horizon.

I follow the crowd of passengers from the bus stop to the square in the centre of town. A cathedral is at one end, the harbour at the other. A few of the other travellers head straight for a restaurant with tables under red umbrellas, and I walk past it, searching each of the faces for his.

I pull at my shirt, trying to separate it from the sweat on my back and stomach. Two men speaking English pass behind me and I turn around, but they're too young.

The harbour promenade isn't crowded, but the bars along it are busy and all of the moorings, just on the other side of the seawall, are taken. I watch the uniformed crew moving around a large yacht.

In the summer, thousands of visitors arrive here to swim and sunbathe and get leathered on rosé. Some of the bars rent sun loungers on stone outcroppings for fifty euros a day. There are parties on the yachts, at villas, restaurants and nightclubs, and beach bars that people swim to from their sailing boats. Even in exile, he's still managed to be at the centre of things.

Then in the autumn the visitors leave and the locals reclaim the town. I think he'd like that part too. It even sometimes snows here in the winter.

A man steps onto the deck of a four-tiered yacht moving across the water, with a phone to his ear, and bounces the flat of his hand on the railing. Past the harbour are the tiny Pakleni islands, more like an exposed reef. I count nine sailing boats floating around them. My father knows how to sail, he might be on one of them.

My hotel is an old stone building off the square. I had to give the receptionist my passport, and she carefully wrote down its number in a ledger. I didn't book one of the rooms with a kitchenette, since I plan to eat all of my meals out, though there's little chance of seeing him in a restaurant, there are dozens in town. I've found the ones that he would probably like—Gariful, DiVino, Dalmatino— but he might prefer to order a plate at a bar, or to cook at home.

I've tried to work out the places most people have to visit regularly in a town this size: the supermarket, petrol station, cashpoint. There's a large cashpoint at the bank on the square, and two petrol stations, both on the road to Stari Grad, but the supermarket seems like the best place to start. There's a Spar on the edge of town and anyone who lives here is likely to visit it often. Even if he pays someone to do the shopping for him, he might still stop at the Spar for incidentals, beer, for example, or soap.

By the time I arrive at the supermarket, it's only an hour from closing but still busy. The doors barely have time to shut between customers. An old woman leaves carrying a pink chicken breast in plastic, then a group of gap-year students with groceries and bags of ice. A few locals stop in on their way home from work, still dressed in hotel and restaurant uniforms. An Englishwoman motions to her bare feet, and waits outside the supermarket while her husband enters. She notices me, and I pretend to also be waiting for someone inside.

The rush slows eventually. Through the glass shopfront, I watch the cashiers stretch their backs and chat with one another. Another customer arrives, and the automatic doors hang open for a moment after he's passed through them.

At nine, a girl leaves her till with a large ring of keys and locks the supermarket doors from inside. I buy a burek from a stall and carry the greasy paper bag to the cathedral steps. The stone facade of the cathedral is lit behind me. A few other visitors sit on the steps, and the smell of weed drifts over. I lick the grease and pastry flakes from my fingers.

At the restaurant on the square, the red umbrellas are all closed, tied with strips of canvas. I can see all of the people at the tables, my father's not among them. Voices and the scrape of cutlery echo around the square. I finish the burek and crumple its oil-stained paper.

A few of the diners pay their bills and the waiters come to clear their dishes. It's after ten. My father's at home now, probably. Reading, maybe, or preparing for bed.

———

A SMALL PEBBLED BEACH lies past the harbour. I sit on the shore with my elbows on my knees while morning sunlight shines through the clear green water. The wind is at my back, lifting glassy clear prongs from the tops of the waves.

No one comes down for a swim. At seven, I stop at a café on the promenade for breakfast and a pot of thick, syrupy coffee. A young woman in a black shift and apron brings it to me. "Have you lived here long?" I ask.

"I grew up in Stari Grad," she says. She barely has an accent. In the high season, she must speak English as often as Croat.

"It's such a beautiful place," I say, and she smiles to herself, as though adding this to a tally of tourists describing her home to her. "Are there many expats here?"

"Some."

"Where are they from?"

She looks to the ceiling, lifts her eyebrows, sighs. I notice that she's written a number on the back of her hand in black marker. "Germany. Holland."

I pour milk into the coffee. "Any Brits?"

"Yes."

"Is there a particular bar they go to? I was hoping to watch the football match tonight."

"They go to all the bars," she says darkly. Not the most polite guests, from what I've read, especially the British students. Across the room, a man in a pink polo shirt is trying to summon the waitress, his finger in the air.

"Have any of the expats been here long?" I ask. She seems willing to continue talking to me, if only to keep the man in the polo shirt waiting. "My friend's uncle moved here," I say. "Maybe you know him. He's English, he must be in his sixties now."

"William?" she says.

I have to clear my throat before I can speak. "That might be it, I can't remember his name. Is he tall?"

She holds her hand flat in the air, below her shoulder, and my lungs deflate. The man in the polo shirt is halfway out of his chair now, clutching his napkin in a fist against his lap. She sighs and crosses the room to him.

———————

THERE ARE LONG GAPS between customers at the Spar, it's not as busy as last night. The day has turned hot and the nails in the bench burn my skin when I brush against them. I want to take a book from my bag, but I might miss him while reading. Some detectives apparently use language tapes while doing this sort of thing. I considered that, or a radio show, an *Archers* omnibus would be comforting. I didn't download any, as a kind of bargain. I'll endure this discomfort, and he'll appear.

I have brought a bag of fruit gums, though, and allow myself one per hour. While people go in and out of the Spar, I explore different ways of eating a fruit gum, sucking, chewing, dissolving, pressing to the roof of my mouth. The bargain was idiotic. I wish I had something to do with my hands. The backpacker next to me on the bus here spent the ride knitting. She seemed to enjoy it, it seemed a nice way to pass the time. Sometimes I stand and do a circuit of the car park, or stretch my arms. Still, by nine my body is aching from spending so many hours on the bench.

My legs float beneath me as I cross the town square. I've barely drunk anything today, and drain a litre of water before reaching the harbour. I press my body to the seawall and look down at the black water between the boats.

He might not even be here. He might not be in Croatia at all. Alice might have told her parents the truth, and they advised her on what to tell me. I might be watching a supermarket in a town where he doesn't live. The memory of how carefully I applied the hair dye at home makes me wince. I put Vaseline along my hairline first, so the dye wouldn't stain my skin, so when we met my father wouldn't know it had been done recently. I took a long time over this, and made sure not to miss any spots.

This is only a more humiliating version of all the other research trips I've taken in the past. To Newhaven, Eton, Rules. When it's over, I'll return home, like I did after those trips, and try to convince myself that I'm making progress.

Last winter I read about a man who was stabbed in the neck by a stranger at the tube station in Walthamstow. He narrowly survived. In an interview afterwards, he said he hoped his attacker received the help he needed. He'd only agreed to the interview to raise awareness of planned cuts in the mental health budget. He said no, he wasn't frightened of using the tube again. Despite the interviewer's best efforts, he showed no signs of being traumatized. He said he'd decided to think of the attack as he would, say, a bicycle accident.

What would my life have been like if I'd made that decision?

33

A LARGE YACHT FLOATS in the deep channel outside the harbour, since it's too wide to fit in the moorings. From the café on the promenade, I watch a motorboat travelling towards it, carving white foam from the blue water. A hatch in the yacht opens, and the smaller boat steers inside. This surprises me, a boat inside a boat. It reminds me of a toy I once had, a stuffed dog with a Velcro tab and puppies inside. I doubt the owner of the yacht would appreciate the comparison.

I return to the bench outside the supermarket and press play on the first of the *Archers* episodes. I have thirteen hours of them downloaded. I've brought a bag of pick-and-mix, too. More flavours, more to keep me occupied as the day wears on.

There aren't many customers, so I spend most of my time watching the road, which leads across the island to Stari Grad, though most of the cars pass too quickly for me to see who's inside.

I'm becoming more convinced that Alice has punished me by

sending me here. I don't entirely blame her, though the idea makes me feel exhausted, enervated. If it's true, then this is probably the first of many punishments. Her parents will want to teach me a lesson, if they know I've been inside their home.

I don't have to stay here and wait. I never bought a return ticket, I can go to the airport tomorrow. Before I left, I prepared my flat for a long absence. I suspended the post, emptied the fridge, lowered the thermostat so the heat won't switch on in a cold snap. I took Jasper to Laila's with a month's supply of kibble and most of his toys. I completed each of those tasks with a sense of purpose. I was being deliberate, like I needed to have all of my affairs in order before what would happen next. I want to crawl out of my skin with the shame of this. A better person would forgive him. A different sort of better person would have found him years ago.

––––––––––

The next evening, a Sunday, the Spar closes early. I wonder if my father attended church this morning. It's one of the questions I've had for ages, if he has given confession, if there's a priest somewhere who has known the truth and decided not to break the oath of secrecy. At times I've hated this imagined priest as much as my father.

At five, a cashier locks the supermarket doors and I return to town. I decide to watch the cashpoint in the square, but after sitting for a moment, I'm on my feet again. I'm too hot, I've spent the whole day sweating. I stop at the hotel for a swimsuit before going to the beach.

I take off my dirty clothes and walk into the water. I swim a few lengths under the surface and chills sweep down my back. I dive down into the cooler channels. The backs of my eyes are indigo, then red as I swim up into the sunlit water. It's clear enough to see the pebbles on the bottom, and the sea urchins. A few fish knife past. I float on my back, and the water lifts me up and down.

I'm far enough out to see other swimmers in coves down the coast. A woman steering a small sailing boat back to the harbour raises her hand to wave to me as she goes past. I swim parallel to the land until my muscles ache.

I start to walk in to shore, then gasp, doubling over. I lift my foot from the water and rest it on my other leg. A black sea urchin spike is sticking from the bottom of my foot. I pull it out, and a line of blood curves over my foot and drips into the water.

On shore, I squeeze my hair into a knot and pull a dress over my wet swimsuit. I should pick up an antiseptic, the splinters can cause infection. I cut into town on the narrow medieval roads. It's Sunday evening, the chemist's might be closed. The bottom of my foot doesn't hurt, exactly, but I'm aware of the place where the spike entered.

I walk past a hardware shop, then turn back. They might have rubbing alcohol. I push open the door, and a man on the other side smiles and steps back into the shop to make room. He reaches to the top of the door to hold it open for me.

I look at him to say thank you, and the sensation is like a hard shove. He smiles and apologizes. Then I move aside and he steps through the doorway. The door swings shut, and he passes on the other side of the glass.

I reach my hand out for balance and knock a box of measuring tapes to the floor. I bend to pick them up, grabbing fistfuls and stuffing them back into the box, and then I'm on the road outside the shop.

Twenty-six years ago, he sat across from me in a booth at Luxardo's, in a dark suit, with the parlour's striped wall behind him. He looks the same, though his forehead is hatched with vertical and horizontal lines, and there are pouches under his eyes.

He's already at the corner. I walk slowly, keeping the same distance between us. A plastic bag from the hardware shop swings from his hand. We walk towards the square on a narrow road, under the stone buildings and red roofs. He takes a canister from the bag and reads its label while he walks.

I look at the back of his head. His hair is silver now. He's wearing a collared shirt with the sleeves pushed up, canvas trousers, and suede boots. He always did dress well. He turns uphill, away from the village, but his stride doesn't change, he's still in good shape. My foot slips. When I look down, there's blood in my sandal, I've left a trail of it behind me.

The road hooks and he passes out of sight. I come around the corner in time to see him climbing into an old desert jeep with cracked leather seats and no roof or doors. I'm close enough to hear his keys clinking before the engine starts, and to see ropes and a tyre iron in the open back.

When the traffic clears, he drives out of the car park and onto a road that leads away from the coast. The jeep thuds as he changes gear. Soon after it disappears from view, its engine changes pitch, like it's travelling uphill. It won't be hard to find him. The roads in that direction end in the hills, they don't cross the island's interior.

Exhaust hangs in the air around me. I listen until I can't hear his car anymore, and the oil dripped on the tarmac has started to dry.

He looks so similar. He's inarguably the same man. But I still can't put them together, my father and the man who came to our house that night. I'd thought that setting eyes on him again might help me believe that he did those things, but it hasn't. He looked so ordinary. While he was walking from the hardware shop to his car, the flat of his shoe caught on the pavement, so he was brought up short. It only lasted a second before he adjusted his balance and continued walking, but I keep thinking about it, it was such a common, clumsy movement.

I find an open chemist's and buy rubbing alcohol and a bandage. In my hotel room, I use the mirror on my compact to see if any of the sea urchin spike is still under the skin. The blood has already soaked into my sandal, and the water in the sink turns red and brown as I scrub at the cork. This seems to take a very long time, but walking across the square and hiring a scooter takes no time at all. A group of American students on the garage forecourt have also hired scooters. They're driving to Milna to watch the sun set. Two of them are nervous, and the man at the garage laughs and says, "They don't go very fast," which is useful to know.

I drive back towards Dolac Road. My sandal's still wet, I can feel it loosening the glue on the bandage. The scooter is low and heavy, the students should have an easy time of it. All of the rentals are the same, which is good, I'll look like any other tourist.

It's seven o'clock. Sunlight glows in the weeds growing around a low barbed-wire fence on the side of the road. As I drive up the hill, the houses become farther apart, and between them are stretches of wild land. The sun is at my back, casting my shadow long in front of me, and I watch it lengthen and slide across the tarmac when the road curves.

There are a handful of houses up here, all built to face the view. One after the other, the houses rise ahead of me, solid, modern concrete blocks set on acres of limestone and shrubs, their windows opaque with the reflected sunset.

Another house rises. When I'm level with it, I turn my head to look down the driveway. There is his jeep, parked under a trellis made of thin branches. His is one of the last houses on the road before it tapers off into scrub grasses at the highest point above the town. Past the end of the road, on the crest of the hill, is a generator in a cement hut. I walk the scooter off the road and sit on the gravel with my back against the generator.

The sea slowly blackens. Lights start to come on in the town. A dog barks somewhere down the hill, and the generator hums behind me. This is his view. It's quite a nice one. In the winter, he'd be able to watch snow fall on the sea. He has a deck, built out from the house on wooden stilts. He may have had it added to take advantage of the view. Or the sunshine, he looks like he's spent a lot of time in the sun.

That's one part of what I gathered from his appearance. The other, more important one is that he seems healthy. He isn't diminished, like James is diminished. He hasn't started to hunch. His clothes fit well, too. He might have found a tailor here, he always bought hand-cut shirts and suits. He's in his sixties now. There are some changes—the hatched forehead, the silver hair—but not many. He walked easily from the hardware shop, the plastic bag swinging from his hand. He looked happy.

At two in the morning, I walk down the hill to his house. A thunderstorm has begun far out at sea. Lightning flashes behind the clouds, so they glow like a smoked mirror.

Some of the houses up here have decals for a security system. His doesn't, though he might still have an alarm. I would, if I were him. A drystone wall separates his property from his neighbour's. From the far side of the wall, I look between the olive trees at his house. I have to be quiet, I'm only about ten yards away from his open windows. I don't know if I can go any closer. Already my heart is jolting, the hairs standing up on my arms and the back of my neck. It's late, though, and the lights have been off for hours. He must be asleep.

The house is more modest than I would have expected. It has smooth, varnished concrete walls and a flat roof with a few vents and a chimney. I'd pictured a swimming pool, after seeing him. He looks like the sort of person who swims laps every morning.

The garden hasn't been cultivated, the land around the house is the same as on the open side of the hill. When I climb the wall and drop down onto his property, the dry grass reaches to my knees. If he's awake, he might be able to hear it crackling from inside.

He has a fire pit, and a grill across it with dark shapes where meat has charred to the metal. A plastic table and chairs are set on the deck. He'd be able to eat his meals outdoors most of the year.

I walk around the side of the house and stumble. Someone is

standing in front of me. I stop breathing. Heat flashes through me, and my legs weaken. He moves closer. Then I notice the laundry cord and choke in air. Not a man. A wet suit, hanging up to dry. It's the long kind, with full arms and legs, and its damp fabric still smells of salt.

I walk, unsteady on my feet, to the trellis and his car. Before leaving London, I visited the electronics department at Selfridges to buy a device. A few months ago, I'd bought one for Laila, since she often loses the key to her bike lock. It's an ordinary key fob, except with a GPS chip. You download an application, type in the code, and the tracker appears on a map. I slide the fob into one of the cracks in the leather, then push until it's wedged against the cushion. I run my hand over the seat. You'd never know it's there.

I hurry down his driveway to the road. When I look over my shoulder, I expect to see him standing at the window, but it's still dark, with only the shapes of the white curtains shifting inside.

I'm not the last person home. Two girls are on the steps of the cathedral with a bottle of vodka at their feet. The square is quiet enough for me to hear the vodka swish in the bottle when one of them lifts it to her mouth.

They wave at a girl walking towards them from the end of the square. The sound of drums comes from one of the bars on the beach. The girl moving towards me is in tight jeans and a black top, her long hair down around her back. They're Italian, I heard the other girls talking. She's wearing a black choker, which in this light makes it look as though her head has been separated from her body. She's walking quickly, on the balls of her feet, and looks like she's about to start laughing. I wonder what she left behind her, and she smiles at me as we pass each other.

I turn off the square, down the narrow lane to my hotel. A few streetlamps shine on the ghostly sides of the buildings, showing the scratches in the white paint on the closed shutters, the dark shapes of the doorways. I normally walk out of reach of doorways if it's late and I'm alone, but tonight I trail my hand against the sides of the buildings.

34

"I FOUND HIM."

On the other end of the line, Nell says to someone, "Sorry, I need to take this." There are muffled sounds, then she says, "Claire?"

"He's been living in Croatia."

"Oh god. He's been arrested?"

"No. I haven't told the police yet."

"What?"

"I want to watch him first." There's silence on the line. I can picture Nell, screwing her eyes shut. "It's all right, he's not going anywhere, this is where he lives."

"Has he seen you?"

"No. He wouldn't recognize me anyway."

"He might. Do you really look that different to when you were little?"

I can't tell her about the hair dye, the eyebrows, the weight. She'd be furious if she knew how long I spent planning this without telling her.

"How did you find him?" she asks.

"I blackmailed someone."

"Oh, Claire."

"I know."

"Where are you?"

"Hvar Town."

"I'm going to call the police."

"You can't, please."

"Why, what are you doing? Are you going to hurt him?"

"No, of course not. I only want to watch him." I need to know who he's been pretending to be, how he spends his time, if he's as happy as he seems. Though it's more than that. I need to know who he is. A good man who did a bad thing. A bad man who's done more bad things.

For years, I've been tormented that the people around him wouldn't know who he was, that they might be in danger. It seemed impossible that I had no way to warn them.

Though maybe I never needed to warn them, maybe I've been wrong about him, and so have the police, and Mum. Something is missing, has always been missing. He wouldn't kill Emma. He had no reason to harm her. The official theory is that he mistook her for Mum at first, but then why wouldn't he stop? There was a bruise on Emma's mouth. He saw her face.

And there's another part that doesn't make sense—he left Mum. He began to find her a bit dull. He'd moved on, according to his friends, according to everyone the police interviewed.

I don't understand why, after leaving, he would go back to kill her.

"How long do you need?" asks Nell.

"A week."

"I'm calling the police in four days," she says.

There is a cove down the coast to the east of town, hidden behind thick cypresses and pines. I'd never have found it if I hadn't been tracking the key fob. The pin on the map started and stopped as he drove here from his house. The fob is still in his car, transmitting its location from the dirt car park behind the cove.

I spread a jute mat on the pebbles. There are a few other people here—a woman sunbathing on a yellow towel, a boy stacking pebbles, a couple reading on their stomachs—though my attention is on the man pushing a Zodiac into the water.

My father steps carefully, looking down to check his footing. There are even more sea urchins here than at the other beach, I can see their black shapes under the green water.

He steps into the boat and pulls a cord to start the outboard engine. A glossy plume of water rises behind the motor. The sea is so calm that instead of leaving a wake the boat scores two lines in the translucent surface. He steers towards the Pakleni islands, where some other boats are anchored, but then the engine stops, and his boat drifts. I have to squint to see him against the glare on the water.

Nothing happens. I wonder if the engine died, but then, instead of trying to restart it, he's feeding an anchor over the side of the boat. He tugs on the rope to check the mooring, then begins to assemble equipment. Soon the top half of his wet suit is fastened, and he has a harness on his back holding an aluminum tank. A tube in his mouth. A mask. He clips a weight belt around his waist, and then he is stepping off the boat into the water.

He's learned how to scuba dive. He must have a lot of practice, to be diving alone. A certificate requires hundreds of hours, but, then, he's had plenty of time.

I watch the flat surface of the water. He's beneath it now, I wonder how far. It's quite a dangerous hobby, scuba diving. So much can go wrong. Decompression sickness, aneurysm, nitrogen poisoning, faulty equipment. And he dives alone, no one would be there to help if something went wrong.

I watch for a while longer, then lie back on the mat, rubbing the line of iridescent sweat in the crease of my elbow. I turn my face to the mat and breathe in its hot straw smell. I wonder if there are sharks in this water.

An hour later, the sunbather sits up on her towel, stretches her neck, and pulls the straps of her swimsuit onto her brown, freckled shoulders. She climbs onto a bicycle at the edge of the dirt car park, the towel draped around her neck. The boy has left too, the only people at the cove are me and the couple, who have gone for a swim and returned to lying on their stomachs. The woman is resting on her forearms, messing her hands in the pebbles, and I listen to their dry rattle.

He still hasn't surfaced. I sit with my arms on my knees and watch the flickering scales of light on the water. The Zodiac looks like it's been floating there for a long time. I can see white rims of salt dried on the black rubber.

I might be keeping him under the surface. The force of my presence on the beach, like a hand on his head in the water.

Then the boat jerks. One violent movement. I shade my eyes against the sun, in case I imagined it, but it jolts again. Sharks under the water, the commotion of them feeding, their backs pressing against the bottom of the rubber boat. Or it's only him, holding on to the anchor rope as he swims to the surface.

His head breaks the water. He pulls himself into the Zodiac and begins to remove his equipment. I don't stay to watch. I need to be by his house before he arrives.

The house across the road from his is a vacation rental. I found its listing online, it's empty this month. It also has a raised deck, with exterior steps and a view onto my father's property. The top of the stairs is partly hidden by a pine tree, and it's just far enough that he's unlikely to see me unless he's deliberately looking. If he does happen to look over, he'll see a tourist, sitting on the steps of her deck, reading. I've brought a book, a lighter, a pack of cigarettes.

When he returns, he's dressed in swimming trunks and a damp linen shirt. I watch him hose down the wet suit. He goes to the car and returns with a chunk of bread, which he tears into while rinsing the rest of the equipment. He must be hungry from the dive.

Bright beads of water drip from the wet suit. He climbs the stairs to his deck. I think he might look over then, but instead he slides open the door and steps into the house. It wasn't locked. And he's left it open behind him.

Inside might be wall-to-wall with guns, but I doubt it. He doesn't seem to think anyone's coming for him, after all these years. He doesn't have an alarm, or if he does he never sets it. The whole property is open. And he moves freely in and out, judging by the shirt hanging over the edge of the deck, the book on a chair, the wooden tongs with leather cords left by the fire pit. The fern that he's taken onto the deck to water, leaving a damp circle on the boards. That he owns a fern is another surprise. It looks quite healthy, too, like he's taken good care of it.

The shirt on the edge of the deck lifts and flattens in the wind. The wet suit begins to dry, matt patches blooming across it, and the entire scene starts to seem artificial, planted. He may have noticed me. He may be inside the house, watching from behind the curtains. I can't figure out the distances. I don't know, if he came towards me, if I'd be able to get down the deck stairs and away in time.

No sounds come from inside his house. Then there's a cascade, and I startle, knocking my elbow against the rail, but it's only him having a shower, the sound coming through the open bathroom window.

Soon after, he steps onto his deck in navy trousers and a white collared shirt, and sits at the table with a book. I don't think he's seen me. He doesn't look over, but it's not practised, he doesn't seem to be avoiding it on purpose. In the distance, the white light of an aeroplane glows against the banked blue clouds, like a beacon on top of a mountain.

A car is coming up the road. I watch it appear and disappear around the bends until it swings into my father's drive. A man gets out and my father comes down the deck stairs to greet him, shaking his hand, holding him by the shoulder.

He's in his fifties, I'd guess. Tanned, with cropped white hair and white teeth. They climb onto the deck, waving when a second car arrives and another man steps out. He's brought a freezer bag of steaks. I can see brown liquid pooling in the corners of the plastic.

The three of them pull chairs around the deck table. They drink bottles of Karlova ko beer and talk in Croat. My father's fluent, apparently, speaking quickly to the others, laughing.

One of the men goes inside and returns with the steaks on a glass tray. They must be good friends to be so familiar with his house. My father arranges charcoal in the fire pit, then pours paraffin over it. Soon smoke lifts from the fire in a tall, twisting column. After the steaks cook, he scrapes the tongs clean on a stone, leaving behind black scorch marks.

They pass salt, pepper, a bowl of roasted potatoes. My father eats briskly, with precise, deft movements. While he swallows, he holds the knife and fork upright on the table. He wipes his hands on the napkin on his lap. The steak is rare, I can see the blood pooling on his plate.

I look at his guests and wonder what these men did during the war. Bubbles form in the bloody grease in the steak pan. I watch one of the guests wash down a mouthful of meat with his beer.

It grows dark, but the men around the deck table are spotlit by a bare bulb fixed under the roof. When my father pushes his chair back from the table, the white napkin on his lap is streaked brown and red.

He returns with a bottle of rakija, the plum brandy I've seen in every restaurant here. The men push away their plates, resting their forearms on the table. I wish I could understand what they're saying. The conversation has grown serious. At one point, my father pulls his hand down his face. One of the other men is shaking his head.

When they finally stand from the table, it's late. Their cars switch on, each headlight illuminating a colourless circle of grass and dirt.

My father is alone inside his house now. I can hear water in the sink, glass clinking. The lights switch off. I wait. Thin smoke still curls from the fire pit. He hasn't cleared their plates. In the darkness, a bird lands on the table and begins to peck at the meat.

He's had a lot to drink. The bottle of rakija is empty, and how many beers before that? Three? He keeps a tyre iron in the back of his car. I could carry it into the house, where he's asleep in bed. He must be drunk enough not to wake at the sound.

I won't, though. Of course I won't. I wasn't lying to Nell. During my training shifts in A and E, I saw the moment someone passes from life to death. I could never do that to someone, not even him.

35

MY FATHER is sitting in the corner of a café the next morning with a tablet, a legal pad, and an espresso. He scrolls on the tablet, taking down notes, reading over a pair of steel-rimmed glasses. I put my phone on the floor, kick it under the next table, then stand, rifling through my bag. "Sorry," I say to him. "Have you seen a phone? I can't find mine."

He lifts his head, with a courteous, reserved expression. I'm aware of my rusty hair, cork sandals, the flesh of my shoulders rounding where the straps of my vest cut into it.

"I haven't, no," he says. He's flattened his accent, so he might be from any number of places. He caps his pen and begins to look around him for the phone. I go to the counter to ask if anyone's turned one in, and the assistant shakes her head.

"Here you are," he says. When I turn around, he's holding it out to me, loosely, between thumb and forefinger.

The shattered screen is a nice touch, I think, for a backpacker.

Genuine, too. I dropped it on the canal towpath a few weeks ago. "Thank you so much."

He says, "Not a problem." His tone is pleasant but clipped, like he's trying to signal that he has to return to work now.

"I'm Sarah."

"Grant," he says.

"Losing it would have been a disaster, I'm only visiting." He nods politely. It's not going to work, we won't fall into conversation, we won't become acquaintances, he won't tell me anything about himself. He's not giving me any openings, and it will seem odd if I try to force it.

He looks at the yoga training book on my table, and his expression turns wry, like he's thinking I'm probably not particularly good at yoga. Next to the yoga book is a large, flaky pastry stuffed with pistachios and honey. No discipline either. "Thank you again."

"You're very welcome," he says, and we both return to our seats.

Grant. It wasn't one of the names I'd imagined, but it suits him. He takes notes from the tablet, and I turn the pages of the yoga book, the paper sticking to the honey on my fingers. I notice that he has a tattoo on the inside of his forearm. A row of Greek letters, which I copy into my book to look up later.

After a half-hour or so, he packs his tablet in a leather briefcase. I recognize its silver buckles and the lock on its flap, I used to play with it. All of his things went to my grandmother after his disappearance. He may have asked James to bring him a few of his favourite belongings after she died, or ordered a new briefcase from the same company. He's noticed me staring, and I turn my face down to the book, to a diagram of a spine twisting, until he's gone.

A few minutes later, I move to the doorway and watch him step into a stucco house down the road. I'd passed it on the way here. It's a reiki centre, with a wind chime above the door, and next to it a box of leaflets about craniosacral therapy.

I've never had a craniosacral massage before, but imagine it as an extended version of when someone washes your hair before a cut. A shivery sensation, lifting the hairs on your arms. The pressure suddenly draining from your head as they press your temples or work their knuckles against the base of your skull. The best sensation in the world, then. I'm always so disappointed when they switch the water back on.

Hollow wooden notes scatter from the wind chime. The blinds are drawn over the windows. He's inside having a reiki session, he's lying on a table in a treatment room while someone massages his head. Or he's having pure reiki, in which the practitioner doesn't touch you but, per the leaflet, circulates your energy. He thinks he deserves this, even after what he did.

In my hotel room, I find a chart online of the Greek alphabet. I open the yoga book to where I copied down his tattoo and match each of the symbols to a letter. It takes me a while. One of the symbols could be a few of the Greek letters, I hadn't been able to see it very clearly. I copy the letters one by one into a translate box. *Eleutheria* is the transliteration. Freedom.

A WASPS' NEST hangs above his yard, a large oval of crumbling grey layers, like papier-mâché. Wasps hum around it. My father is standing under the nest, shaking a canister. I lean forward from my position on his neighbour's deck to see around the scrim of pine needles. A metal ball clicks inside the canister as he shakes it. He aims the nozzle and a jet sprays against the nest, foaming on its surface. I read once, on the sort of site I used to visit, that you should carry wasp poison instead of mace, since its spray can reach twenty feet.

The wasps leave the nest, a glittering cloud of them lifting above the tree. My father climbs a stepladder under the branch, holding a baseball bat. A few last wasps still hover around him. He might be allergic to their stings. He might not know, most people aren't tested for it. His blows land with muffled thuds, until the nest splits from the branch and falls to the ground.

An hour later, I walk down his driveway, past the empty trellis. The jeep's gone. He took it into town, according to the signal from the key fob. The wasps' nest is still on the ground, split open into segments of ashy grey chambers.

A smell of paraffin rises from the fire pit. Pieces from some project are on a work table in the grass. He's left out a saw, with a stretched wire instead of a blade, like a larger version of the one we used in pottery class at school. I remember how easily the wire sliced through clay.

I climb the deck stairs and slide open the glass door. He has a wooden dowel to lock it from inside, but it's leaning upright against the wall. I pick it up, even though I know it's unnecessary—he's in town, I watched him leave, and the key fob will tell me if he's coming back—and carry it with me through the rooms.

My father stayed in a house in Laurel Canyon once. Decades ago, but it must have made an impression. He has the same low wooden chairs and rush mats. On the windowsill is a handful of rough pink quartz crystals. I read the titles on his bookshelf, upset to see we've read some of the same ones. The house has a distinct smell, deep and loamy, that I can't place.

The other room is even more spare. A bed, a desk facing the sea. A laptop is open on the desk, with a black screen. I feel too jittery to go through it yet, but force myself to sit down. The wooden dowel is slick with my sweat. I rest it against the desk and wipe my hands on my jeans.

I open the spreadsheets and documents saved on his desktop. It takes me a while to work out what they are. He trades index funds. For himself, and some clients, through a shell company, presumably, registered offshore. So this is how he's supported himself. He seems to specialize in clean energy.

His email account won't load without a password. I open his browser history for the past three months, as far back as it goes, and take pictures of it.

His kitchen is at the other end of the main room behind a polished stone counter. I open the fridge. All of the shelves are wiped clean, the food neatly arranged. A plastic tub with "BEEF BROTH" written in marker on a piece of masking tape, black garlic, a jar of white miso paste.

I open the cabinets. Glassy panes of dried seaweed. Maca powder, cordyceps, bee pollen, spirulina, chaga. The tops of the bags are folded over and held with bright plastic clips. I remove the clip on the bag of mushroom tea. That's the smell throughout the house, that wet-earth smell.

He can't get this stuff in town, he must have to order it online. It makes me furious. All this care in tending to his body, when Mum and Emma have nothing, can experience nothing, because of him.

I've been in his house for over an hour now, and it's started to seem like he's never coming back. The jitteriness is gone, replaced by a sort of trance. There's no wind, everything in and out of the house is still.

I take my time. There is a safe in his wardrobe. A small one, but large enough to hold documents, cash, a gun. I try a few combinations, without success. I'm checking the map for the location of the key fob less and less often.

I've been in his bathroom for a while, sifting through blister packs and prescriptions. Nothing unusual. An expired antibiotic, melatonin capsules, aspirin, toothpaste. On its side, hidden behind the antibiotic, is a tube of lipstick.

I twist it open. The lipstick is light pink and has been used often. Someone's mouth has shaped it into a crescent.

I go back through the rooms. Nothing else, though, that clearly belongs to a woman. No shoes or hairpins. No notes or photographs. The lipstick is an odd shade of pastel pink. The sort of colour someone young would wear.

I replace the dowel against the wall. The wood is still damp from my sweat. I like the idea of him noticing that, mystified and unsettled.

I'm tempted to leave something else behind. I could unscrew the lid from one of his jars and leave it out on the counter, so he couldn't be sure if he left it there or if someone else was inside the house. But it would only harm me, in the end, to warn him about what's coming.

I close the door and turn away. There's a clatter from inside as the dowel falls into the runner. I push at the handle but the door doesn't move, of course, it's locked from inside, the dowel holding it in place.

I circle around the house. The front door is the only other entrance, and it's locked. I shove my shoulder against it, then look at the map. The pin is moving. It must have been moving for a while, actually. He's already at the base of the hill.

I can hear an engine. The muscles tense at the back of my neck and sweat prickles across my skin. I pelt up the road. When I hear his car behind me, I force myself to slow to a walk. The engine grows louder. He should have turned into his drive by now, I think, he must have gone past it. My ears pin back.

But then there's the sound of gravel churning, and when I turn around he's pulling in to the driveway. I duck behind the generator as a car door slams. I wait until after the sweat has dried on my skin, then climb onto the scooter and drive down the hill.

He must have seen me walking on the side of the road. Which would seem odd, there's nothing in this direction, the road ends at the top of the hill next to the generator. But seeing a woman walking near his house, and the door being locked from inside, can't be enough to make him run. Maybe the woman was on her way to hike round the back of the hill, maybe the dowel slipped on its own.

Was there dirt on my sandals when I went into the house? Did I put the food back in the right order? I wasn't careful. I can't believe now how uncareful I was.

I don't remember putting the lipstick back in the cabinet. I remember taking it out and looking at the colour, but not replacing the cap. I might have left it out on the sink.

———————

AT THE HOTEL, I run a cold shower. I'm in a towel, combing my hair, when my phone rings.

"Claire Alden?"

"Yes," I say, and the telescoping begins, the numbness, bracing for what I'm about to hear about my brother.

"I'm calling from Penbridge. Your brother's here."

"What?"

"He arrived this afternoon. He won't have his mobile for the first week, but you can call this number if it's really urgent."

She asks if I have any questions about the twenty-eight-day programme. My face is wet, and it's like a soft avalanche, all through my body.

"Do you need my bank information?"

"He wants to pay for it himself, but we do need a guarantor."

"Yes, of course."

After the call, I rush down the stairs and onto the cobbled streets. The buildings are tabbed with open shutters, and I look up at them as I walk, brimming with the news.

I can go home now. There's a small police station in Hvar Town. They might make the arrest, or Interpol might send officers. But once I do that, it's over. His house will be cordoned off and he'll be in custody. I'll only get the scraps that come out in police statements or during the trial. It won't be like this.

At eight in the evening, the pin for his key fob starts to move. If he drives towards Stari Grad and the ferry, I'll call DI Tiernan, but the pin stops in a car park behind DiVino. When I walk to the harbour, my father is having dinner on the restaurant's terrace. He's wearing a heavy silver watch and a shirt with the cuffs folded back. His friend—another man, about his age—is separating the bones from a whole grilled fish.

I stay behind my father. I'm in different clothes now, but he must have noticed me on his road, I can't risk him seeing me again. I watch as he talks with his friend and uses a fork to dig the meat from a bowl of mussels. I want to know if he ever thinks about his son. If he ever has a sense of how much Robbie has suffered.

His friend gestures at the large yacht anchored in the channel, and my father turns to look at it, his face in profile, his chin resting in his hand. I heard two tourists talking about that yacht yesterday, saying that its windows are made of bulletproof glass. I wonder what the owner has done to make that necessary, and watch as my father's friend pours them both more wine.

36

A T THE HOTEL the next morning, I type in another address from his browser history, which opens a discussion thread on pu-erh tea. I'm halfway through the history now. He visits forums and news sites often, on diving, mostly, and nutrition, some political ones. He checks the weather and the surf report, to plan dives, probably. He seems to be considering the purchase of a sailing boat.

I type in one address and a video loads. It's not porn, exactly. Two women sit on a bed in gingham dresses, touching each other's arms and hair. Their dresses lace up the front, and they pull at the ribbons, which are like white shoelaces, before the video abruptly ends.

A handful of names appear in his search history. Most of them are his clients, I recognize them from the documents on his desktop. Three, though, don't seem related to his work. I've heard of the first one, the heir to a Greek shipping firm. His yacht has visited Hvar Town, maybe they've met, maybe he's a potential client. The second is a farmer in North Yorkshire. The third is a nurse in Boston, Tessa Martin. Her name sounds familiar, but I can't remember where I've heard it.

There isn't much about her online. The fundraising page from a race she ran, a blurry picture from a work holiday party, a profile for the clinic in Boston with a small headshot and a list of her qualifications. BSc. King's College London 1974, Oxford University Merton College 1968–70. I read through it again. Tessa went to Oxford, but didn't graduate. She left after two years and finished her degree in London. Before that, though, she was in the same year as my father and his friends.

I can't decide whether or not to call her. She might be close to my father, she might warn him after we speak. Though that seems unlikely. Why would he have looked up a friend's name twice in the last month? Especially when there's so little about her online.

With the time difference, I have to wait until the afternoon to call. When a receptionist answers, I say, "May I speak with Tessa Martin?"

"She's not available. Are you a patient?"

"No, a friend. Can you please ask her to call me?" I give her my number and say, "My name's Lydia Spenser."

Half an hour later, my phone rings. "This is Tessa," she says. She still has an English accent, even though she's lived in America for years.

"Thank you for calling me back," I say. She waits for me to continue. She recognized my name, she hasn't asked how we know each other. "I don't really know where to start. My father's Colin Spenser. Do you know him?"

"Why?"

"I found your name in some of his things."

"Is he dead?" she asks.

"No," I say, and she falls silent. "I'm trying to understand what happened in my family. If you did know him, I won't tell anyone."

"Are you a reporter?"

"No."

"Can you prove it?"

"My mum would be sixty-two on December the second."

"You could have looked that up."

The trouble is so much has been published about us, there's little I know that a stranger couldn't. "When he was at Oxford, my father loaned his car to his friend Sam Brudenell, and Sam was in an accident on the Abingdon Road."

Tessa breathes in sharply. "How old are you?"

"Thirty-four."

"I've always wondered what happened to you and your brother." Her voice has an echo now, like she's gone into a different room. I answer her questions about where we moved afterwards, how we've stayed anonymous.

"Why would my father search for your name? How did you know him?"

"I had a tutorial with Sam," says Tessa. She stops and clears her throat. "He asked me out to his friends' party. There were fifteen of us, the eight Ramsden Club members, me and six other girls.

"Sam was making the drinks. We were all dancing. I remember being sick in the room, in front of everyone. I was so embarrassed, but Sam was nice about it, he wasn't angry. He said I should go and lie down. I fell on the stairs and he helped me the rest of the way. He said he was going to get me some water.

"When I woke up, my clothes were on the floor. There was some blood on the sheets. It was light outside. When I went downstairs, they were all in the sitting room, still drinking. James asked if I wanted an orange juice."

I listen with a hand over my mouth, and my legs shaking enough to make my shoes rattle against the floor.

"I told the university," says Tessa. "Sam came to my room that night and said no one would believe me, he'd talked to the other girls at the party and they would swear that I was making it up. When I went back to see the chancellor, I thought she would try to convince me not to drop the complaint, but she didn't, she knew who Sam's family was."

"So you left?"

"No, I wanted to stay, I loved Oxford. I left in the next term, after I heard what had happened. It wasn't only Sam, it was all of them."

I bow my head against the dizziness.

For so long—not only as a child, even recently—I've made up reasons for what he did. He'd taken something on the night of the murder, or had a psychotic break. Something in him had come loose momentarily, but the real version of him was the one I'd known, not the version who came into our house that night.

But there was never another version of him. I understand that now. He didn't have a double life. No one does, there's only ever one. The man in the attacks is the same one who taught me to read is the same one who raped another student.

"Have you told anyone?"

"My husband and son," says Tessa. There's a pause, and then she says, "I told your mum."

"What?"

"She came to see me after they separated. She'd heard Colin say my name on the phone, she thought we were having an affair. When I told her, she couldn't speak. I held her hand. She asked me what I wanted to happen to them, and I said I wanted them to be punished."

Her voice clots, she's started to cry. "She went to ask your father about it, and took a tape recorder, to show the police. He denied it, so she bluffed. She told him she had proof, he couldn't lie about it anymore."

"Why didn't she tell the police during the inquiry?"

"I begged her not to. I was scared, I thought I'd be next. I can't tell you how much I wish I'd never told her. I think about Emma every day."

I've wanted to know his motive for so many years. My father planned to kill Mum because she'd found out about Tessa. There's no statute of limitations on rape, he might have gone to prison. Along with Sam, and James, and the rest of their club, the members of Parliament, bankers, judges.

There's a relief in knowing the truth—a completion, a block finally dropping into place—but I'm also so stricken it hurts to breathe, and weeping, my face hot, my hands clutching my stomach. I'd thought there might still be a way out of this. A notch in the circle through which all of us, even him, could escape.

*

I press a cold towel to my swollen face. I stand at the window and watch people walking in the alley below the hotel. I think of his clipped plastic bags of maca and dried mushrooms. The sunlight on the pink quartz crystals. I wonder if he believes in their healing powers. He owns a meditation pillow. Which means he can close his eyes at will, and feel peace.

37

M Y FATHER and a mechanic are on the garage forecourt. His jeep is levered up on a pole inside, they seem to be discussing a repair. The mechanic holds his hands apart to demonstrate a size, and my father nods, with his arms folded over his chest. He seems nonchalant. It's an old car, it must need repairs often.

The two of them crouch underneath the chassis. After a while, they reappear on the forecourt. The mechanic offers him a rag and my father wipes the black grease from his hands. He does this for a long time, working the rag around each finger, even after they must be clean. That was one of the things his friends said in his defence, I remember. That he was particular, that he didn't like to be dirty, that he couldn't be around blood.

My father shakes hands with the mechanic and walks back towards the centre of town. I take out my phone and call DI Tiernan. It goes to her voicemail. I call the other number she gave me, for her department at the Met, and the receptionist puts me through to another detective in her unit. He knows who I am. As soon as I tell him my name, his voice loses its boredom and impatience.

"DI Tiernan gave me her number, but her mobile is switched off. Do you know how I can reach her?"

"She's on a flight," he says. "I can help in the meantime."

I don't know anything about this man, I don't know if he'll do this correctly. The police have let my father escape before.

"That's fine. Do you know when she lands?"

"Not for another five hours," he says. He's curious, he wants me to tell him instead of waiting. "She's coming from Singapore."

I thank him and end the call, cursing. Without the key fob, I have no way of knowing where my father is. I circle through town, past all of the places I've seen him, the reiki centre, the café, the restaurant, the hardware shop, but he isn't at any of them. He might stay up at his house until the car is repaired. He might be enjoying the break in his routine, the excuse for laziness. I try not to panic. He hasn't been warned, he has no reason to leave now. DI Tiernan will land soon, it's only a few more hours.

I walk to the cove hidden down the coast from town, where my father went scuba diving. The sun has just dropped below the horizon, but there's still light in the wide dome of sky. I fold my dress on top of my bag, then pick my way over the shadowless beach. Everything is clear, poised, held in the same even light.

The water's warmer than the air. The rocks shift under my feet, and I look down to avoid the sea urchins. The water closes around my hips, then my waist. I float my palms on the surface, stirring

247

them so ripples spread around me. My dry hair brushes against my back. A few birds fly over my head, towards the Pakleni islands.

There are no other swimmers. Behind me, the dirt car park is empty of cars. I dive under the water, and shivers crest over my scalp. I tread water for a long time, facing the horizon, the salt keeping me buoyant. Then I turn to head back in.

A man is standing on the shore.

The cove is surrounded by boulders. I'll have to come in near him. It's fine. It's still light. And there are people on a boat nearby, if anything happened they'd hear me.

I swim back in, turning my head from side to side. I walk the last few steps, waves foaming around my legs.

My father is standing a few yards from my bag. I smile at him, and he nods in return. His feet are bare, and I notice the knobs of bone on their sides. He's wearing the navy swim trunks and a white linen shirt.

He doesn't turn to watch me walk past. He's not here because of me, I think, with relief. He comes to this cove often. I pull my dress on over my bathing suit. My feet are numb, I can't get them into my sandals, they keep sliding off.

"Did you have a nice swim?" he asks.

"Yes." My voice sounds distant. He still has his hands in his pockets, but he's looking at me plainly. My scalp tightens. I understand now. He's seen me. He knows I was inside his house.

The boat isn't in view anymore. It's gone back to the harbour, we're alone. He must think I've stumbled on him, and plan to sell the story to a newspaper, or blackmail him.

"Are you done swimming?" he asks.

I don't answer. I don't run or start screaming, because doing either would be like giving a signal for it to start. And because part of me is expectant, like I'm about to learn the answer to a question.

I won't tell him who I am. It doesn't matter, does it? If he would make an exception. I want to know what he would do to a stranger.

I bend down to pick up my bag. I give him a polite smile and start towards the car park. Then he's at my back, and the fear is like a hood dropping down the length of my body. I've only taken a few steps when his hand closes around my wrist.

He drags me to the water. It splashes up my front as I try to twist away from him. I'm not screaming, but my breath is rasping.

We've been here before. When I was four, maybe, or five, we stood in the warm shallows off a coast, and he said, "Can you swim to me from there?"

His hand is still around my wrist, but he's looking at me. He's not just looking at me, I realize. He recognizes me. He knows who I am. I understand this, and then the panic booms through me.

"No," I say, "no, Dad."

He takes hold of my hair and pushes my head under the water. My eyes are open, but I can't see anything, only the water churning. Pressure tightens in my throat and the bottom of my lungs.

It's loud under the water, with the rocks shifting under his feet. I dig my nails into his hand to loosen his grip, and he jerks my head hard, so my neck twists. The back of my head burns where my hair is being pulled out. I breathe in then, and water rushes up my nose. The pressure in my lungs is worse now, and my chest is convulsing.

I open my eyes again. The water is still churning white. He can't see my hands. I run them over the pebbles until I feel a cluster of sharp needles. I break off one of the spikes. Then I stop resisting, and let him hold me under the surface. The water starts to clear, streams of air moving to the surface.

As soon as I can see, I push the sea urchin spike into the soft web of skin between his first and second toe. It slides in easily.

He grunts and lets go of my head. I rear back, so I'm squatting in the water. He reaches for his injured foot, his brows drawn together, his mouth open in disbelief.

He's a tall man, it seems to take ages for him to bend forward. I stand, lift a rock with both hands, and bring it down as hard as I can on the top of his head.

His full weight falls forward, onto me, and I shove him off. I thrash away from him. My feet slip, and my arms jerk in the air to keep me upright. I stop, panting, with wet hair scraped over my face. Water and spit roll down my chin.

He's face down in the water. I wait for him to stir. I'm still holding on to the rock, so hard that blood starts to drip between my fingers. He isn't moving. I flinch, dropping the rock, wiping my red hands on my dress.

My heart stamps, and I look towards the shore. There's no one in the dirt car park or between the pines. In the distance, a water taxi is speeding towards the harbour, but it's too far away for me to see the people on board, they won't be able to see me either.

Small waves move past us. Water slides under his shirt, lifting it from his back, and then it's gone, and the wet fabric plasters to his skin.

I don't know how many times I watch this happen. The sky has faded more, leaving a tarry darkness under the pines, though it's still light. Anyone on shore would be able to see us. I hold my shaking hand at my mouth.

I force myself to move closer, and check for a pulse. He doesn't have one, I knew he wouldn't, and my body's trembling now. I only hit him once. There isn't any blood on his head or in the water around him. He looks like he could still stand up.

Something has happened to time. Everything seems to be moving slowly, but with blank spots, so I don't remember where I was standing or what I was thinking a moment ago.

My body's cold. I need to get onto shore, and walk to the police station in town. I finally start wading in, then stop. I look at my hands and arms, touch the back of my head. There are no bruises. He was trying to drown me, but that hasn't left a mark. No one witnessed it. And I came here to find him. They might not believe me that it was self-defence.

I clutch the wet fabric of my dress and bend in half, something howling through me. This can't have happened, this can't happen, I can't go to prison.

I lift my head and look at the cove. He was going to drown me. What was he going to do with my body? The lot is empty. He didn't bring his car, or the Zodiac. The town is a mile or so to the west, and to the east is wild coast, the waves foaming against boulders, with tall pines above them. No houses, that I can see.

I step forward before I can think about it. I hold the back of his shirt and start to drag him through the water, towards the rocky coast to the east. I don't think about his face, I don't look down.

My arm and shoulder start to ache, but I have to bring him further away from the town. I keep expecting to hear the bump of a speedboat on the water, or sandals on the rocks above me, for people to suddenly careen into view. We're so close to the shore.

Farther down the coast, a pine tree has fallen into the water.

Waves sluice over its dark trunk. Once I'm finally past it, I scan the boulders, until I notice a gap between two of the rocks.

I flip him over and start to unbutton his shirt. He can't be wearing a shirt, it has to look like he was swimming. The buttons keep catching on the wet fabric. My throat heaves, but then it's done, and I slide it off him. I bunch the shirt around my hands so I won't have to touch his skin, and push him until he's in the narrow space between the boulders.

A wave comes from behind us, and there's a loud thunk as it pushes his head against the rock. The wave recedes, dragging at his body, then he's pushed against the boulder by the next swell. By the time he's found, his body will be covered in bruises. The one from me will be camouflaged by the others, and by then I'll be far away from here.

I pull myself out of the water and up the rocks, strip off my wet dress and bundle his shirt inside it, and carry them in my fist through the trees.

It's nearly dark when I reach the cove. My sandals are at different places down the beach, where they tore from my feet as he dragged me. I look at their pale shapes in the dim light.

He would have collected my sandals from the beach after he killed me. He would have taken them somewhere to burn or bury. They're only cork, they would incinerate or decompose quickly, and no one would have ever known where I'd gone, my brother would have never known.

Neither of the straps is broken. I fit the sandals onto my feet, and they carry me off the beach.

38

WHEN I CAME HOME from the airport, I slept for sixteen hours. I ordered a takeaway, then another, and another, since I was constantly starving. I showered often, dyed my hair back to its natural colour, and waited for the story to appear in the news.

His body was found six days after my return to London. It was ruled a drowning. There was no inquest, it's a common cause of death on the island. There are twelve drownings a year off the Dalmatian coast, on average.

The funeral has already happened. He was buried as Grant Holleran. He would hate that, he would want to be restored to his rightful name and buried in England.

DI Tiernan returned my call when I was on the ferry. We'd just left Hvar, I could still see the lights on the island. I panicked, like she'd be able to see me, and the stained clothes in my bag. I went out on the deck in the darkness, the inside of the cabin a fluorescent box behind me, with a few people inside it. She said, "I got your message. Is everything all right?"

"I thought I saw him."

"Where?"

"Hampstead Heath."

She asked me a few more questions, but her voice was gentle, conciliatory, like she didn't believe I'd seen him, or that he'd ever be found.

"It probably wasn't him," I said. "It was probably a stranger."

I left his shirt in a bin near the port on the mainland, and my stained dress in another bin in a different neighbourhood. Even if there had been an inquest, no one in Hvar would ever connect it to me. My father made sure of that, no one there knew who he was.

The Frasers know, of course, and Sam, but they won't ask the police to look into it. An investigation might show they'd been in contact with him. They might even be relieved. What they did will stay hidden now. Alice might have told her parents about me, but our secrets are evenly weighted, none of us will talk.

Alice did send me a bill for the cancelled party. It was waiting with the rest of my post when I returned from Croatia. I posted her a cheque, though so far she hasn't cashed it.

It's over, nearly.

THE DRIVE to Yorkshire takes five hours. After Hawes, I pull off onto a single-track road. The leaves have changed colour. It's autumn now, it seems like it hasn't been autumn in ages. I drive farther north, across the dales. Sheep gather on the side of the road behind a crooked wooden fence, and horses stand in a field under heavy green blankets. I pull into a gateway when another car comes past. Oaks and chestnut trees arch overhead, and acorns crack under the tyres.

A painted wooden sign for the farm hangs above its gate. After parking on the grass, I walk past tables laden with crates of apples and jugs of cider. I stop a woman in a green fleece. "Is Mark here?"

A man comes outside in a flannel shirt and down gilet. He has short hair and brown eyes with sun lines around them. He looks younger than I expected, even though I found his age online. He's only forty-six.

He shakes my hand. "You're here about the caravan?"

"No. Do you have a minute?" I wasn't sure before, but his expression confirms it. He knows exactly who I am, he's been waiting for me.

As we walk towards a bench on the far side of the barn, he asks me where I drove from, in a casual voice, but I saw his face a moment ago, he was terrified.

We sit down at the edge of the orchard. A cider smell comes from the fallen apples. "I'm Colin Spenser's daughter," I say.

Mark won't look at me. He hunches over his knees, the heels of his hands pressed against his eyes.

"My father died recently."

"What happened?" asks Mark.

"He drowned."

Mark slumps against the bench. "Do you want me to turn myself in?" he asks.

"No. I know you have children." He huffs then. He has two

teenage daughters, Sophie and Meg. "I want you to tell me what happened."

"He said I'd be saving you," he says.

"How did you meet?"

"At a pub in Kilburn, when I was twenty. I wasn't doing very well." I don't ask what he means. He has a public record, he was arrested for possession of amphetamines, the first time when he was eighteen. "I was at the pub every day, he started to come in often, and we talked."

"What did you talk about?"

"Football, mostly, at first. Politics, music. He asked about my family. I liked talking to him. I didn't have many friends."

"What was your family like?"

"I grew up in care."

That's it, then. That was why he was chosen.

"He told me about his family. He said that he and his wife were separated and she had custody." He stops for a long time then, his head tilted back, his mouth opening and closing. "He said she abused you."

"What?"

"He said she made fun of you, from the beginning. He said after he moved out, he started to notice bruises on both of you, and burn marks. He tried to get custody, but the judge gave you to your mother during the separation, he said fathers almost never win their cases. He said he wanted to run away with you both, but was scared he'd be caught. He came in one night in tears, and showed me a picture of his daughter with scrapes on her arm. He said he'd taken it to the police and they still wouldn't do anything."

"When was this?"

"The first week in November."

"I fell off my bicycle in November," I say. "I had to go to A and E."

I don't remember my father taking the picture. He may have done it when I wasn't looking. Mark is crying now, screwing his thumbs into the backs of his eyes.

"How did he ask you to do it?"

"He didn't ask, really. He said she was going to end up killing the children, and then we were talking about what night. He said he'd pay me. He gave me the information for a savings account and said he'd put twenty thousand pounds in it, but I wasn't going to collect the money. That wasn't—"

"I believe you."

"I was supposed to meet him afterwards in Eaton Square. I was nervous. I hadn't slept in a few days, and bought an eighth of meth. It was more than I'd ever done before, I was out of my mind." His eyes are cracked with red. "I saw the woman's face afterwards. It wasn't her. I thought I'd gone into the wrong house."

"Did you hear another woman?"

"No."

"Did my mum see you?"

"No, I don't think so. Colin must have realized something was wrong when I didn't meet him. I'd come late, too, he must have been waiting for a while. He came into the house and told me to get out."

Mum didn't lie, then. My father came up from the basement and started to beat her. She didn't know another man had been in the house.

"I went to the police station the next day. I was going to tell them everything, but I couldn't go inside."

257

"Did you ever speak to him again?"

"No. How did you find me?"

"Your name was in his search history. He might have been worried you'd confess."

His body is shuddering now, and the bench shakes beneath us. Mark was younger than Emma at the time. "She would forgive you," I say.

I don't know if this is true. I try to decide as we say goodbye, as I walk to my car and drive away. I think she would agree with me that the important thing now is his daughters. Sophie and Meg. It can't all start over again, for them this time.

———

WHEN I ARRIVE at Penbridge, Robbie is at the bottom of the garden, playing chess with another of the rehab residents. I watch for a while. Robbie is laughing, and they talk steadily as they play. They seem to be friends. When he looks up, he notices me without surprise. He says something to his friend, and crosses the lawn.

"Robbie," I say. His face is calm and steady, like he already knows the ending of the story I'm about to tell him.

39

I STAND AT THE EDGE of the loch and pull up my wet suit. I had to order a special one to fit me now. As I wade in, my body is warm inside the wet suit, even in the icy water.

The loch is mercury-coloured and ringed with black mountains. It's spring now, you can tell there was snow here not long ago. On shore, Jasper is sitting on his haunches, near the tent where Nell is still sleeping. We're in the Highlands. Nell chose Glen Lyon for the shape of the loch and the mountains, and the ring fort nearby.

I dive under the surface. I haven't developed a fear of holding my breath, after what happened. Other things have become difficult. There's a particular sound, a hollow thud, like rocks hitting each other, that I can't stand. And I don't wear my hair back anymore, since it can feel like a hand pulling on it.

But the sea doesn't alarm me, which is good, since I see it so often. I moved to Edinburgh three years ago. My flat's on Windsor

Street, at the base of Calton Hill. Every morning, I take the dog up the hill. From its crest, I can see the roof of the practice in Stockbridge where I work. The view stretches over crooked lanes of stone houses, bridges, chimneys and warehouses to the Firth of Forth.

I paddle across the loch. Mum was right about swimming while pregnant, I do feel like a submarine.

Liam has been one of my best friends since I moved to Edinburgh. He's a GP in Leith, we met at a training day. We went out a few times last summer, before settling back into friendship. In October, I asked him to meet me at a restaurant in Merchiston. "I'm pregnant," I said. "It was an accident. I don't know if you remember, there was that time when—".

"Is it mine?" asked Liam, his Scottish accent booming through the restaurant.

"Yes, but I don't expect anything, you don't need to be involved."

"Can I be involved?" he said. He was beaming. "I didn't think I could have children." We stayed talking at the restaurant until it closed.

Last weekend, I found the diagram of Mum's family tree. I carefully taped it to the wall, and drew a new line to the place where, in two months, I'll write my daughter's name.

For now, though, we're in a loch, in spring, under a white sky and black mountains, and both of us are kicking.

ACKNOWLEDGMENTS

THANK YOU TO:

Lindsey Schwoeri, my editor, for bringing your enormous talent, creativity, and skill to this book. You've been wonderful at every stage, and I'm very grateful.

Emily Forland, my agent, for being both tremendously kind and a razor-sharp reader and guide.

Allison Carney, Gabriel Levinson, Lindsay Prevette, Gretchen Schmid, Andrea Schulz, Kate Stark, Brian Tart, Olivia Taussig, and everyone at Viking Penguin.

Federico Andornino, Rebecca Gray, Lynsey Sutherland, Steve Marking, Craig Lye and all at Weidenfeld & Nicolson.

Michelle Weiner at CAA.

Michael Adams, Marla Akin, Debbie Dewees, James Magnuson, and the Michener Center for Writers and Yaddo.

Dr. Noelle Quann, for talking to me about being a GP.

A *Different Class of Murder* by Laura Thompson and *Trail of*

Havoc by Patrick Marnham, two fascinating studies of the Lucan case.

My friends, and especially Nick Cherneff, Kate DeOssie, Donna Erlich, Jackie Friedman, Allison Glaser, Lynn Horowitz, Allison Kantor, Suchi Mathur, Justine McGowan, Madelyn Morris, Althea Webber, and Marisa Woocher.

My family, and especially Jon Berry and Robin Dellabough. And Jeff Bruemmer.

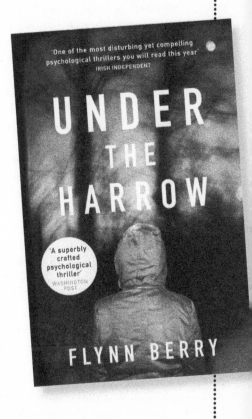

1

A WOMAN IS MISSING in the East Riding. She vanished from Hedon, near where we grew up. When Rachel learns of the disappearance, she will think it's him.

The hanging sign for the Surprise, a painting of a clipper ship on a green sea, creaks in the wind. The pub stands on a quiet road in Chelsea. After finishing the job on Phene Street, I came for lunch and a glass of white wine. I work as an assistant to a landscaper. Her specialty is in meadows. They look like they haven't been landscaped at all.

On-screen, a reporter moves through the park where the woman was last seen. Police and dogs fan out across the hills behind the town. I could tell Rachel about her tonight, though it would ruin our visit. It might not have anything to do with what happened to her. The woman might not have even come to harm.

The builders at the house across the road have finished eating, the white paper bags balled at their feet, and are leaning back against the steps in the cold sunshine. I should have already left for the train to Oxford, but I wait at the bar in my coat and scarf while a detective from the station in Hull asks the public for any information about the disappearance.

When the broadcast moves to the storm in the north, I leave under the hanging sign and turn on the next corner toward Royal Hospital Road. I walk past the trimmed squares of Burton Court. Past the estate agent's. Sunny homes in Chelsea and Kensington. I still live in a tower block in Kilburn. The stairwell forever smelling of fresh paint, seagulls diving at the balconies.

I don't have a garden, obviously. The cobbler's children have no shoes, etc.

Black cabs drive down Sloane Street. Blurry orbs of light glow on the sides of buildings, reflected from the facing windows. The bookshop displays a pile of new translations of *The Thousand and One Nights*.

In one of the stories, a magician drank a potion made from a herb that kept him young. The problem was that the herb grew only at the top of a mountain, and so every year the magician tricked a youth into climbing the mountain. Throw down the herb, said the magician. Then I'll come and get you. The youth threw down the herb. I can't remember the end. That may have been it. I've forgotten the ending for most of the stories, except the important one, that Scheherazade lives.

A few minutes on the tube, and then I am back out again, hiking up the stairs to Paddington station. I buy my ticket and a bottle of red wine at the Whistlestop.

On the platform, the train engines hum. I wish Rachel would move to London. "But then you wouldn't get to come here," she says, and I do love her house, an old farmhouse on a shallow hill, with two ancient elms on either side of it. The sound of the elms soughing in the wind fills the upstairs bedrooms. And she likes living there, living alone. Two years ago she almost got married. "Close brush," she said.

On the train, I press my head against the seat and watch the winter fields pass by the window. My carriage is empty except for a few commuters who have left work early for the weekend. The sky is gray with a ribbon of purple at the horizon. It's colder here, outside the city. You can see it on the faces of people waiting at the local stations. A thin stream of air whistles through a crack at the bottom of the pane. The train is a lighted capsule traveling through the charcoal landscape.

Two boys in hoods run alongside my carriage. Before I draw level with them, they jump a low wall and disappear down the berm. The train plunges through a tight hedge. In summer, it turns the light in the carriage green and flickering, like being underwater. Now, the hedge is bare enough that the light doesn't change at all. I can see small birds in the gaps of the branches, framed by vines.

A few weeks ago Rachel mentioned that she plans to raise goats. She said the hawthorn tree at the bottom of her garden is perfect for them to climb on. She already has a dog, a large German shepherd. "How will Fenno feel about the goats?" I asked.

"Demented with happiness, probably," she said.

I wonder if all goats climb trees, or only certain types. I didn't believe her until she showed me pictures of a goat balanced at the edge of a fan of cedar, a group of them in a white mulberry. None of the pictures showed how the goats climbed the tree, though. "They use their hooves, Nora," said Rachel, which doesn't make any sense.

A woman comes down the aisle with a trolley and I buy a Twix bar for myself and an Aero for Rachel. Our father called us greedy little girls. "Too right," said Rachel.

I watch the fields trundle by. Tonight I'll tell her about my artist's residency, to start two months from now in the middle of January. Twelve weeks in France, with lodging and a tiny bursary. I applied with a play that I wrote at university called *The Robber Bridegroom*. It's embarrassing that I haven't done anything better since then, but that no longer matters because in France I will write something new. Rachel will be pleased for me. She will pour us a celebratory drink. Later, over dinner, she will tell me stories from her week at work, and I won't tell her about the missing woman in Yorkshire.

The train sounds its horn, a long, low call, as it passes through the chalk hills. I try to remember what Rachel said she would cook tonight. I see her moving around in her kitchen, shifting the massive slate bowl of chestnuts to the edge of the counter. Coq au vin and polenta, I think.

She likes to cook, partly because of her job. She says her patients talk all the time about food, now that they can't eat what they want. They often ask what she makes, and she likes to give them a good answer.

Clay roofs and chimney pots rise above a high brick wall

alongside me, and then it wraps around, enclosing the village. Past the wall is a field of dry shrubs and hedges with a few paths tunneling through it. At its edge, a man in a green hat tends a bonfire. Charred leaves rise on the drafts and spin into the white sky, floating over the field.

From my bag, I take out the folder of properties to let in Cornwall. Over the summer, Rachel and I rented a house in Polperro. Both of us have time off at Christmas and plan to book a house this weekend.

Polperro is built into the folds of a coastal ravine. White-washed houses with slate roofs nestle in the green rivulets. Between the two cliffs is a harbor and, past a seawall, an inner harbor, large enough for maybe a dozen small sailing boats, with houses and pubs built to the water's edge on the quay. When the tide is out, the boats in the inner harbor rest on their hulls in the mud. On the western hook of the ravine are two square merchant's houses—one a tweed-brown brick, the other white. Above them, umbrella pines stand outlined against the sky. Past the merchant's houses, on the point, a fisherman's croft is built into the rocks. The croft is made of rough granite, so on foggy days it blurs into the stones around it. The house we rented was on a headland ten minutes' walk along the coast path from Polperro and included a private staircase with seventy-one steps built up the cliff from the beach.

I loved Cornwall with a mad, jealous ardor. I was twenty-nine and had only just discovered it, but it belonged to me. The list of things I loved about Cornwall was long but not complete.

It included our house, of course, and the town, the Lizard Peninsula, and the legend of King Arthur, whose seat was a few miles up the coast at Tintagel. The town of Mousehole, pronounced "mouzall." Daphne du Maurier and *Last night I dreamt I went to Manderley again*, and of course you did, anyone who left here would. The widow's walks. The photographs in pubs of wrecks, and of townspeople in long brown skirts and jackets, dwarfed by the ruined hulls.

Every day the list had to be rewritten. I added the umbrella pines and the Crumplehorn Inn. Cornish pasties and Cornish ale. Swimming, both in open water and in the quiet, dripping caves. Every minute, really, even the ones when we were asleep.

"Everything's better here," I said.

And Rachel said, "Well."

"What's your favorite thing about Cornwall?" I asked, and she groaned. "Or I can tell you mine."

But then she said, "Well, to start, there's the sea."

If anything, she loved it more than I did, and she is even more excited than I am to go back. She hasn't been herself lately. She seems frayed by her work, and always tired.

At the next station, the conductor warns the passengers of possible delays tomorrow because of the storm. Excellent, I think, so it is going to snow.

We pass through another town, where the cars now have their headlights switched on, pale yellow marbles in the weak afternoon light, and then the train curves around a poplar hedge and straightens as it pulls into Winshaw.

Rachel isn't at the station. This isn't unusual. Her shifts at the hospital often run late. I leave the platform under a light so dull that the roofs of the town already seem to be dusted with snow. I walk away from the village toward her house, and soon I am on the open stretch of the road, a narrow tarmac ribbon between farms.

I wonder if she is walking to meet me with Fenno. The bottle of red wine thumps against my back. I picture Rachel's kitchen. The bowl of chestnuts, the polenta bubbling on the hob. A car drives toward me, and I step onto the verge. It slows to a crawl as it approaches, and the woman behind the wheel nods at me before accelerating down the road.

I walk faster, my breath warming my chest, my cold fingers curled in my pockets. Heavy clouds mass overhead, and in the quiet the air takes on a tinnitus ring.

And then her house is in sight. I climb the hill, and the gravel crunches under my feet. Her car is parked in the drive, she must have just got home. I open her door.

I stumble back before I know what is wrong with the house, like something has flown at me.

The first thing I see is the dog. The dog is hanging by his lead from the top of the stairs. The rope creaks as the dog slowly rotates. I know this is bad, but it is also amazing. How did you do that, I wonder.

His lead is wrapped around a post on the banister. He must have tangled it and fallen, strangling himself. But there is blood on the floor and the walls.

I am hyperventilating, though everything around me is calm and still. It is urgent that I do something, but I don't know what. I don't call for Rachel.

I climb the stairs. There is a stripe of blood on the wall just below my shoulder, like someone sagged against it while climbing. When the stripe ends, there are red handprints on the step above it, and the next step, and then on the landing.

In the upstairs hallway, the stains turn messy. I don't see any handprints. It looks as though someone crawled or was dragged. I stare at the stains and then, after some time, I look down the hall.

I can hear myself keening as I crawl toward her. The front of her shirt is black and wet, and I gently lift her onto my lap. I put my hand to her neck, trying to feel her pulse, then lower my ear to her face to hear her breathing. My cheek brushes her nose and chills sweep down my neck. I blow air into her mouth and pump on her chest, then stop. It might cause more damage.

I bend my forehead to Rachel's and the hallway goes dark. My breath rolls on her skin and into her hair. The hall closes around us.

My phone never has service in her house. I'll have to go outside to call an ambulance. I can't leave her, but then I am stumbling down the stairs and through the door.

As soon as the call ends, I can't remember what I said. There is no one in either direction, just her neighbors' houses and the ridge behind them, and in the humming quiet I think I can hear the sea. The sky roils above me. I look up. Put my hands to my head. My ears ring as if someone is shouting very loudly.

I wait for Rachel to appear in the doorway. Her face confused and exhausted, her eyes fixing on mine. I am listening for the soft pad of her footsteps when I hear the sirens.

She has to come downstairs before the ambulance arrives. It will be finished when someone else sees her. I beg her to come down. The sirens grow louder, and my ears lift away from my jaw like I am grinning. I watch the door for her.

And then the ambulance is in view, racing down the road between the farms. It comes up her drive, gravel spraying from its tires, and when the doors open and the paramedics run to me, I can't speak. The first paramedic enters the house and the second asks if I am wounded. I look down, and my shirt is stained with blood. When I don't answer, he begins to examine me.

I pull away from him and run up the stairs behind the first paramedic. Rachel's face is turned to the ceiling, her dark hair pooling on the floor, her arms at her sides. I can see her feet, in thick woolen socks. I want to crawl around the woman and squeeze them between my hands.

The paramedic points at a place on Rachel's neck, then touches the same place on herself, under her jaw. I can't hear her over the sounds I am making. She helps me down the stairs. She opens the ambulance doors and settles me on its ledge and puts a foil wrapper around my shoulders. The wet on my shirt turns cold and plasters the fabric to my stomach. My teeth chatter. The paramedic switches on a fan so heat pours from the ambulance behind me, warming my back, escaping in vapors into the cold air.

Soon patrol cars arrive, the police in black uniforms gathering on the road and coming up the lawn. I stare at them, my eyes streaking from one face to the next. Static crackles from someone's belt. I wait for one of them to smile and give the game away. A constable lowers a stake into the dirt and runs tape across the door, the ribbon bobbing up and down as it unspools behind him.

The edges of my vision go soft, then disappear entirely. I am so tired. I try to watch the police so I can tell Rachel what this was like.

The sky foams, like the spindrift of a huge unseen wave is bearing down on us. Who did this to you, I wonder, but that isn't the important thing, the important thing is that you come back. At the house across the road, the open barn where they usually park is empty. An Oxford professor lives there. "The gentleman farmer," Rachel calls him. Beyond the professor's house, the ridge is an almost vertical cliff face, with steep paths cut into the stone. I stare at the ridge until it seems to come loose and start to drift closer.

No one goes into the house. They are all waiting for someone. The constable who ran the tape stands in front, guarding the entrance. In the paddock next door to the professor's house, a woman rides a horse. Her cottage stands behind the paddock, near the foot of the ridge. The horse and rider gallop in a great circle under the darkening sky.

As the woman leans forward into the wind, I wonder if she can see us. The house, the ambulance, the uniformed police standing on the lawn.

A door slams at the bottom of the driveway and a man and woman step onto the gravel. Everyone watches the pair advance up the hill. They both wear tan coats, their hands in their pockets, their coattails blowing behind them. Their gaze is trained on the house, then the woman looks in my direction and our eyes catch. I am buffeted by wind, cold air. The woman lifts the tape and enters the house. I close my eyes. I hear footsteps approaching on the gravel. The man kneels down next to me. He waits.

Color sweeps over my eyelids. It will settle soon to black, and then I will hear the elm trees soughing overhead. If I go down the stairs, I'll see our dishes in the sink and on the hob. The scrapings of polenta dried to the bottom of the pot. The chestnut skins on the counter, dropped where we pulled them off, burning our fingers.

If I go to her room, I'll see the shadows of the southern-planted elm flickering on the boards. The dog asleep, sprawled below the bed, near enough that Rachel can drop her arm over the edge of the mattress and pet him. And Rachel, asleep.

I open my eyes.

2

THE MAN KNEELING NEXT to me says hello. He is holding his tie against his stomach. Behind him, the wind flattens the grass on the hill.

"Hello, Nora," he says, and I wonder if we have met before. I don't remember telling anyone my name. He must know Rachel. He has a large, square face and hooded eyes, and I try to place him at an event in town, bonfire night or the fire brigade fund-raiser. "DI Moretti. I'm from the station in Abingdon."

It is a blow. He has never met her, her town doesn't have murder detectives. To file any serious complaint you probably have to go to Oxford or Abingdon. As we walk down the drive, two women in white forensic suits pass us on their way to the house.

As we drive away I can't breathe. I look out of the window at the line of plane trees flashing past. I would have thought it would feel like a dream but it doesn't. The man driving next to me is real, the landscape outside the window is real, and the wet sticking my shirt to my stomach, and the thoughts coiling through my head.

I want the shock to buy me a little more time, but the grief is already here, it came down like a guillotine when the woman put her finger to Rachel's neck. I keep thinking how I am never going to see my sister again, how I was about to see her. As we drive through Winshaw, I realize that I am talking to myself in my head. No one else is there. Usually when I have the uncanny sensation of watching myself think, I shape my thoughts into things to tell Rachel.

I shrink against the seat. Cars rush past us on the dual carriageway. I wonder if the detective is always such a slow driver, or only when he has someone else in the car. I realize I haven't been watching the road signs to check where he is taking me. Part of me hopes he will take me to a dark, wet field, far from the lights of the town. It would be symmetrical. One sister murdered and then the other, in the space of a few hours.

He did it. Then circled around the house and came up the drive, and convinced me to leave with him while everyone else was distracted. It isn't hard to persuade myself. The fear is already here, pressing under the surface. I take a pen from my bag and grip it under my thigh.

I wait for him to ease onto one of the turnings, for an abandoned factory, or an empty orchard. Dead space surrounds the road, he has a lot of options. I ready myself to stab the pen into his eye, and then run back to her house. Rachel will be sitting in her living room. She will look up, frowning. "Did it work?"

But the sign for Abingdon appears, and the detective turns off the dual carriageway, slowing to a stop at the end of the slip road. His face is slack, his eyes trained up through the windscreen at the signal.

"Who did it?" I ask.

He doesn't look at me. The indicator ticks in the quiet car. "We don't know yet."

The signal changes and he pulls the car into gear. The light box sign of the Thames Valley Police revolves on a post at the entrance to the building.

In an open-plan room upstairs, a fair man with a dark suit hanging from his shoulders stands in front of a whiteboard. When he hears us enter, he shifts away from the board, where he has just taped up a picture of Rachel.

I groan. It is the picture from the hospital website, her oval face framed by dark hair. Her face is so familiar it is like looking at myself. She is paler and has stronger bones in her face. I can disappear in a room, she can't. Both of us have high cheekbones, but hers turn out like knobs. She smiles in the photograph with her mouth closed, her lips pressed a little to the side.

In the interview room, Moretti sits down across from me, unhooking the button of his suit jacket with one hand.

"Are you tired?" he asks.

"Yes."

"It's the shock."

I nod. It's strange to be so tired, and also so scared, as if my body is asleep but receiving electric jolts.

"Can I get you anything?" he asks. I don't know what he means, and when I don't answer he brings me a tea that I don't drink. He hands me a navy sweatshirt and tracksuit bottoms. "If you'd like to change."

"No, thank you."

He talks for a few minutes about nothing. He has a cabin at Whitstable. It is beautiful, he says, at low tide. He makes me nervous, even while talking about the sea.

He asks me to tell him what I saw when I first entered the house. I can hear my tongue lift from the bottom of my mouth with a click before every answer. He rubs at the back of his neck, the weight of his hand pushing his head down.

"Do you live with her?"

"No, I live in London."

"Is it common for you to be there on a Friday afternoon?"

"Yes. I often come up to visit."

"When was the last time you spoke to your sister?"

"Last night, around ten."

The sky has darkened, so I can see the pale citrine squares of office lights across the road.

"And how did she sound?"

"Like herself."

Above his shoulder, one of the yellow tiles clicks off. I wonder if he thinks I did it. It doesn't seem likely, though, and my fear of it is distant, another depth charge but one that barely reaches me. For a moment, I wish I were being framed. Then, what I felt now would be something else—worry, outrage, righteousness—other than this. Which is nothing, like waking in a field with no memory of how you got there.

"How long will this last?" I ask.

"What?"

"The shock."

"It depends. Maybe a few days."

In an office across the street, a cleaning woman lifts the cord of a vacuum and shifts chairs out of her path.

"I'm sorry," he says. "I know you must want to go home. Have you noticed anything weighing on Rachel recently?"

"No. Her work, a little."

"Is there anyone you can think of who might want to harm Rachel?"

"No."

"If she felt threatened, would she tell you?"

"Yes."

None of this is like her. I can just as easily see the other outcome. I can see Rachel, drenched in blood, sitting in this chair and patiently explaining to the inspector how she killed the man who attacked her.

"Did it take a long time?" I ask.

"I don't know," he says, and I bow my head against the ringing. The woman who came up the drive with him opens the door. She has a soft, pouchy face and curling hair pulled back into a knot. "Alistair," she says. "A word."

When he returns, Moretti says, "Did Rachel have a boyfriend?"

"No."

He asks me to write down the names of the men she dated in the last year or so. I print each letter neatly, starting with the most recent and going back sixteen years, to her first boyfriend in Snaith, where we grew up. When I finish the list, I sit with my hands curled on the table in front of me, and Moretti stands near the door with his heavy square head bent to the paper. I watch to see if he recognizes any of the names from other cases, but his expression doesn't change.

"The first name," I say. "Stephen Bailey. They almost got married two years ago. She still saw him sometimes. He lives in West Bay, Dorset."

"Was he ever violent toward her?"

"No."

Moretti nods. Stephen will still be the first person to eliminate. The detective leaves the room, and when he returns his hands are empty. I think of the pub this afternoon, and the missing woman in Yorkshire.

"There's something else," I say. "Rachel was attacked when she was seventeen."

"Attacked?"

"Yes. The charge would have been grievous bodily harm."

"Did she know the assailant?"

"No."

"Was anyone arrested?"

"No. The police didn't believe her." They would allow that she had been assaulted, but not in the way she described. They suspected that she had tried to rob or solicit someone and been violently rebuffed. They were the last of the old wave of policemen, preoccupied with the amount she'd had to drink, and that she didn't cry. "It was in Snaith, Yorkshire. I don't know if they still have a record of it. It was fifteen years ago."

Moretti thanks me. "We need you to stay in the area. Do you have anywhere to sleep tonight?" he asks.

"Rachel's house."

"You can't stay there. Is there someone who can come and pick you up?"

I am so tired. I don't want to try to explain this to anybody, or to wait in the station for one of my friends to arrive from London. When the interview ends, a constable drives me to the only hotel in Winshaw.

I hope we crash. A lorry holding metal poles drives in front of us on the Abingdon Road, and I imagine the nylon ribbon snapping, the metal poles falling out, dancing on the road, one of them pinioning me to the seat.

Winshaw high street is curved like a sickle, with the common at one end and the train station at the other. The Hunters is at the bottom of the sickle, next to the train station. It is a square, cream stone building with black shutters. When the constable drops me at the hotel, there are a few people waiting on the train platform, and they all turn to look at the police car.

At the Hunters, I lock the door and put on the chain. I run my hand along the papered wall, then press my ear to it and hold my breath. I want to hear a woman's voice. A mother talking to her daughter, maybe, as they get ready for bed. No sounds come through the wall. Everyone's probably sleeping, I tell myself.

I turn off the lights and crawl under the blanket. I know what's happening is real, but I do keep expecting her to call.